TO THE LAND OF THE CATTAILS

ALSO BY AHARON APPELFELD

Badenheim 1939
The Age of Wonders
Tzili: The Story of a Life
The Retreat

TO THE LAND
OF THE
CATTAILS

Aharon Appelfeld

Translated by Jeffrey M. Green

GROVE PRESS
NEW YORK

Grove Press
841 Broadway
New York, NY 10003

Library of Congress Cataloging-in-Publication Data
Appelfeld, Aron.
To the land of the cattails.
I. Title.
PJ5054.A755T58   1986   892.4'36   86-9076
ISBN 0-8021-3359-2 (pbk.)

Manufactured in the United States of America

Designed by Ronnie Ann Herman

10   9   8   7   6   5   4   3   2   1

TO THE LAND OF THE CATTAILS

CHAPTER ONE

They traveled southward, and their destination was the river. It was a broad land, dispirited, overcast by high mountains like clouds. Now, after the harvest, the region seemed even more wretched, emptiness breathed in it, and the first marks of autumn already nestled in the corners of the fields. But the roads were still dry, thick with dust from the commotion that had held sway all summer long.

"Darling," said the mother in a theatrical voice, "you must suffer your mother's whims, even though you are innocent. For you've done nothing wrong."

The son did not budge; he had stopped reacting to her chatter. It was a strange amalgam of memories, heartfelt yearnings, and scraps of quarrels. From time to time a single word would slip out of her mouth, a distillation of her suffering, but mostly it was monotonous, meaningless verbiage.

"Didn't you hear me?"

"I heard you."

It had been easier in the mountains, but the mother was drawn to the river as if by strong cords, so that they rolled and rolled until they reached that exposed plain upon which the summer's end called down its curse of dust.

"In a little while we'll reach the river." She spoke as she would speak to him when he was a child, to console him or temper his impatience. "The river is absolutely lovely."

"What does she want?" he thought. His attention, though, was concentrated on the horses. Since morning neither oats from the feedbag nor water from the bucket had passed their lips, but how could he stop them in this swamp of dust? He urged them on with all his restrained annoyance.

In the afternoon they glimpsed the riverbank beyond the brush. The mother straightened the upper part of her body and, with a kind of pretentiousness, announced: "I told you. You didn't believe me."

The son knew that it wasn't she, but something within her. She deserved pity, but even so he couldn't help fixing her with an angry stare.

"Don't you see?" she insisted.

She had been born on the banks of that river, and she had never forgotten the blue flame on its waters. During his childhood, before he fell asleep, she used to tell him of the wonders of the River Prut. Over the years the hue of those marvels had changed, but she always spoke about the river with feeling. Once those memories had had a charm that would penetrate his sleep and provoke subtle sensations within him. After awhile the charm wore off.

Now the horses occupied his thoughts. They had been bought just two weeks before, and already he felt a slight, warm affinity for them. "You love the horses more than me," the mother said hastily. She exaggerated, as was her wont, though there was a bit of truth in what she said. More and more he sought their company. They were a pair of fast, shapely horses that had climbed up the mountains with straight backs and devoured the plains. For a moment he imagined he saw the transmigrated souls of ancient knights in them, but he immediately rejected the idea, the way one rejects superstitions.

"Isn't that a unique river?" She was always lavish in her descriptions, but that sentence sounded utterly false to him. The river was meager, and on its banks sprouted a jumble of cattails and river plants devoid of beauty. The water stood low as it does in streams at summer's end.

"What do you see that's beautiful in it?" he said to provoke her somewhat.

"Don't you see? It's natural. Human hands haven't plundered its banks. True, it doesn't enchant the eye, but that is how it left the hand of the Creator."

That answer was unexpected. Such moments of clarity showed, more than anything else, that not only confusion dwelt in her soul.

In the depths of his heart he loved her. He could not fail to love her. She was his mother, who, from his childhood, had lavished tenderness upon him. True, too many good intentions are burdensome, but she was his mother nonetheless, his parent, who offered him moments of grace before he fell asleep, with soft strokes and whispers that would surround his slumber. Were it not for the bad dreams, the nights would have passed like a halcyon cruise in the depths, from which one emerges in the morning altered and purified. The nightmares did more than a little damage. But there were also clear moments, on the rear balcony, for example, between the light of day and the light of evening, when the fence would sparkle with crimson, and the last leafy shade huddled on the steps and quickly gobbled down the red glow.

He often forgot those moments of grace. His mother went to some pains to spoil his hidden love for her. Of course, *her* life had been no bed of roses. His father, August, had divorced her when she was twenty. That gloomy episode had lasted three years, and its traces still had not been erased. Because of him she had left her homeland, her father, her mother, her sisters, and like a fool had followed him to a foreign country. She had sought freedom and found a prison. All the way to Austria he had behaved like a gentleman. But when they came to the city, he removed the mask from his face: a gentile through and through. The handsome young engineer, the polite music lover, beat her roundly even while she was pregnant. Her pleas fell on deaf ears.

She recited her pain to Rudi morning and night, in great detail, at the dinner table and at his bedside. Those descriptions imbued him with disgust for his father and pity for his mother.

Afterward there was no lack of event and scandal in the mother's young life. Though she did not remarry, every year a new love bloomed, a new madness. He learned to observe her with tolerance. As if she were not his mother, but rather some capricious creature that had to be watched patiently. "Why are you looking at me?" She was sometimes alarmed by his stare, his narrowed eyes.

"Nothing, nothing."

"Don't pass judgment on me in anger."

"I?"

He loved to look at her because she was beautiful. But that beauty was her undoing. Men were drawn to her like flies, and she, with great foolishness and weakness, would be seduced, suffer, and at last come home, pretending nothing had happened.

Over the years he learned the map of her face, including all its lightest creases. When he was a boy he would sit for hours and look at her shifting expressions. He also loved to watch her in her sleep, as if she were not his mother, so familiar to him, but one of the wonders of the world that must be observed with diligence. In time his view was spoiled, and he understood that nothing would come of all the promises, wishes, and dreams. Every love affair ended in quarrels and tears. More than once she returned scratched and bruised. Wonder of wonders: she had the power to renew herself, to forget, and to begin again. In his youth he had already noticed those gifts, but only in the school did he realize their full extent.

Finally good fortune favored them. One of her lovers, an elderly man, left her a legacy. She was so happy she broke into tears of joy. The poor woman did not know the full value of the legacy. Soon it became clear to her that it was valuable property.

That wealth, which brought her such happiness at first, afflicted her with melancholy in the end. For a year strange humors seethed within her. In the morning she would buy a dress, and in the evening she would curl up like a cat next to the oven and smoke cigarettes. At the year's end she announced: "We must go."

"Where?"

"Home. The time has come to return home."

With that impulsiveness he, too, was freed: from schools, the quizzes, and the examinations. The slow squeeze, prolonged over eight years, finally sent forth a pale creature from its walls, docile and fussy. Suddenly it was as if that fear had never existed. No more cramming, scrambling, pretending, and anxiety. From now on it would be only he and his mother.

For a few days they traveled by train. It was a waking dream: fears fell away, their eyes absorbed only water and trees, and the more they absorbed them, the more anxiety abated. Even here there was no lack of confusion and delay, but his mother

was as indomitable as a lioness. Something within her, something stronger than she, drew her on. "Home," she said to
one of the border inspectors. "Don't you understand?" The
inspector stood dumbstruck. There was such desire in her voice.

Thus they came to the hinterland. The hinterland is always provincial, even when events in the metropolis already
stomp like violent horses. In the provinces the trees and the
water dominate. The peasants teach their children the ancient lesson: there is nothing new under the sun. There is no
reason to be excited. Rulers come and go, the world stays the
same.

It was the end of summer 1938, but here everything was
as it should be, quiet and idle. As if the plains held out as
much time as you please on the palms of their hands.

When the inspectors at the border check-points heard that
Toni spoke Ruthenian, their eyes lit up. Toni's feelings were
stirred and she was confused as she stood beside the gate and
announced that she was happy to be returning to the land of
her birth. The policemen quickly took note of her beauty and
bantered with her. In her great excitement Toni was calm,
and she paid them back in their own coin.

"Whose lad is that?" asked one of the middle-aged policemen.

"Mine, can't you see that he's mine?"

"Strange," said the policeman, "he doesn't look like a Jew."

"What are you talking about?" Toni said. "If the mother
is a Jewess, isn't her son a Jew?"

"You're right," said the policeman, abashed.

The entire land of her birth lay spread out before her, but
Toni was in no hurry. She sat and chatted with the guards.
The guards, for their part, were not stingy with their compli-
ments. Toni told them at length about everything that had
happened to her in faraway Austria. As if they were not po-

licemen, of whom one must be wary, but elderly uncles, from whom you need hide nothing. Not far from the police station they bought the horses and carriage. Toni did not bargain and paid in cash. The two horses were young and shapely, and Rudi fell in love with them at first sight.

Before they parted the horse trader said, "The lad knows horses."

"How can you tell?" Toni was surprised.

"I can see."

"I," Toni said in a thoroughly feminine way, "do not see." Toni was happy, as only she knew how to be. Afterward they sat in a tavern. Here, too, Toni did not mind her tongue. She asked questions, but mainly she told. The mistress of the house, a fat, strong woman, said, "If it weren't for what my eyes see, I would swear that you were a native Ruthenian."

What marvelous foolishness, a warm torrent of repressed love burst forth from within him. Toni was thirty-four at the time, of medium height, with long chestnut hair. In her high-heeled shoes she looked younger.

True, over the years he had built up no small store of criticism. He used to examine her sentences under a magnifying glass. He found too many contradictions in her behavior. But most painful of all were the lovers who popped up, taking her from him. True, he had nannies, even young nannies, but none of them had his mother's liveliness.

"Isn't it wonderful to return home?" she suddenly broke into his thoughts. "Stupid, why didn't I do it years ago? Because of a little shame, a person does not return home. I should have been whipped." Her hesitations were forgotten, her fears, and, most of all, money. Poverty had oppressed her all those years, and hardest of all was the winter: money to buy coal. Her final suitor, the old man, had shown up only during the past year, and it was he who had turned the tables.

"Home, darling, we're going home. I can't grasp that myself. I'm stupid. Let's hope they still dwell in the land of the
living." She rarely used the expression "the land of the living," only on especially festive or mournful occasions, always
giving it some excessive significance. At times she had what
he would contemptuously call "attacks of faith."

From time to time he would ambush her and, with great
arrogance, disconcert her: "You are a believer," For a moment, she would lower her head, but, recovering quickly, say,
"Certainly I am a believer. No one will take away the faith I
received from my father and mother."

"But you . . . how should I put it?" he would jab.

"That does not matter. I am ready to die for my faith."

He would mock her beliefs and call them superstitions, but
in his heart he knew this was part of her charm.

At the end of August they came to Ozrin, a town consist-
ing of a single street, enveloped in ancient trees that cast their
thick, leafy shade over the yards. The owner of the hotel sat
in the entrance dressed in a white suit. No one was to be seen
in the street, only silence interwoven with coolness. "Have
we reached Ozrin?" Toni asked herself. The hotel owner heard
her whisper and said, "Who do I hear?"

"Are we in Ozrin, I asked."

"Indeed, my lady, indeed."

Immediately the mistress of the hotel, her daughter, the
porter, and a young Ruthenian servant girl appeared in the
doorway as if they had been expecting their arrival for hours.
"My name is Toni Strauss," Toni announced. "And this is my
son, Rudi."

From then on the procedure was simple. The porter took
the suitcases out of the baggage compartment and drew the
carriage into the courtyard. The Ruthenian servant girl picked

up a heavy valise in each hand, as if they were not overloaded luggage but merely bales of feathers.

The owner of the hotel marched in front to show them to their room. It was old-fashioned, simply furnished, shadowy and fragrant with the scent of wood: it had two wide beds and a writing table near the window. The standing lamp had a rustic shade, which, for some reason, made Rudi think of long winter nights, books, and honeycakes.

"Sophie will help you," said the owner of the hotel as he slipped away from the door. "A fine room, a pleasant room," said Toni, looking longingly at her son. Sophie put the suitcases down. "Thank you, Sophie, you have been very helpful." Sophie did not move. Toni, seeing the maid's embarrassment, said,"Excuse me, do you speak German?"

"No Madam. I speak Ruthenian."

"In that case, let us speak Ruthenian. I was born in this region and the Ruthenian tongue is not foreign to me. Ruthenian is a fine language, I grew up with Ruthenian girls. A person must speak his own language." The more Toni spoke, the more Sophie blushed. "Thank you," she said, and slipped away.

The late-afternoon light filtered into the room. Not a sound was to be heard, only the breathing of the beams.

"It's good we've come back," said Toni. "I am very content that we've returned. A person must, in the end, return home."

"We are still far away." In his distraction Rudi was caught up by the talk.

"I don't think we are."

"We can do it all at once. The horses are nimble and game."

"But I'm afraid."

"What are you afraid of?"

"My parents. They won't forgive me. You must stand by me."

"Of course I'll stand by you."

"In that case, I have nothing to fear. If you stand by me, I have nothing to fear. I knew you would stand by me."

They took their supper on the balcony. The mistress of the hotel had gone to the trouble of preparing a corn and cheese casserole for them. Toni confessed, "You are bringing my beloved childhood back to me all at once."

"How is that?" The mistress of the hotel was surprised.

"You must know, Madam, that I am from this region. Now I am returning from exile, a lone exile, and I know how to judge a dish by its color. By sight alone I can testify that it has turned out well."

As if by magic the balcony, surrounded by green vines, evoked old, forgotten, provincial times, times in which a person could wrap himself, as in a sheepskin cloak, and doze off.

"We're going out," Toni announced. Rudi got to his feet, searched his mother with an earnest, cold look and said, "I'm ready."

"To be here for twenty years and not to budge. You understand," she said when they reached the street.

"Yes, why do you ask?"

From time to time a certain suspicion of him would arise in her. She searched his face for his father's evil features, but they seemed to evade her eyes. He was smarter than his father, more restrained: it was hard for her to resist his intelligence. He never asked a simple question: if he did ask something, it was to perplex her, to sow some fear in her, or to confront her with her contradictions, for she did not lack contradictions. Nonetheless her heart exulted: he was not like his father.

They walked along the street. The low houses exuded an

evening tranquility. People were sitting on their verandas, drinking coffee and sharing impressions. The evening light was soft and restful. Here and there an animal cried out, not loudly.

"What could I write to them?" The words broke out of her.

"No one will find you guilty," he said, knowing that in her fear she acted and thought like an adolescent girl.

"It's good that you, at least, understand me."

She had always been frightened, but now her fright had become more comprehensive. The straits were approaching. Soon would be the shore, the sharp headlands.

"Have I ever spoken to you about the faith of the Jews?"

"Only once, I think."

"I ought to sit down and tell you. It is a great faith, a redemptive faith.

"And you believe in the faith of the Jews?" In his usual way, he sharpened the scalpel.

"Certainly. I am a Jewess. Have I ever, in all my days, denied that I am a Jewess?"

"No," he said, to avoid an argument.

"You, too, my darling, are a Jew. True, your father was a Christian. But according to our faith you are a Jew. Because your mother is a Jewess. You understand."

"Clearly," he adopted a neutral tone.

"The Jews, you should know, are a noble race. None of them would beat his wife, remember that."

Meanwhile the darkness descended. Lights were lit in the low, separated houses. But the dim horizon kept dispersing its glowing blue. From the lake a wild shriek suddenly rose and banished the silence. But the evening was stronger than all the voices seeking to break out. Silence again covered the wide space with a thick down quilt.

When they returned to the hotel, the common room was lit and two Ruthenian waitresses served coffee, cakes, and cheese. The light returned to Toni's face, she joked with one of the waitresses and asked her if they had dances at night. One of the guests, an elegant old man, joined them at their table. It turned out he had not been born Christian. His father and progenitor had had him baptized when he was still a boy, but since he had lived all his life among Jews, he had acquired their language and idiosyncrasies.

Toni's face was calm, and she asked for details about the place and the surroundings. The old man told her at length about everything that had befallen him from the day of his arrival there as a lawyer; and he admitted that if he were younger he would return to the faith of his fathers. Now he did not wish to make his daughters unhappy, for they were married to landowners.

"Are they anti-Semitic?" Toni asked in a whisper.

"Of course. And how!" he whispered back.

They both chuckled as if together they had unearthed some secret.

That conversation dampened Rudi's spirits. He observed the lawyer's gestures. Were they reckless or innocent? The truth of the matter was that he was pleased with his mother for bringing the old man to make that confession. Toni was all exaltation and high spirits, and, with a fine feeling of joy in her heart, she said: "Leave those goyim alone. Pack your bags and come with us."

"You are very right," said the old man.

"Of course I'm right," she said haughtily.

Afterward she sat at the bar and drank beer. She told a few salty jokes. When Rudi saw she was going too far, he said, "Tomorrow we have a long way before us."

"Why are you in a hurry?"

"We must not be late," he said, knowing that she would not catch the meaning of his sentence in any case.

"They're always rushing me along," she said, walking behind him.

The next day the light was mottled and the bright sky was covered with clouds. Premature autumn. The owner of the hotel stood in the doorway and apologized. "I did not cause the skies to darken." Forest winds stirred from their lairs and flooded the street. Toni wiped her brow and asked, "Where am I? What in God's name are we doing here?"

"Mother, I instructed the porter to prepare the carriage. The chambermaid has brought our suitcases down. Don't worry. Everything is ready for the trip." That assurance soothed her face for a moment, but not her hands. In her right hand she held a bank note, and asked, "Whom do I owe?"

"The porter, of course, in a moment."

"Shouldn't we give something to the chambermaid?"

"We'll give her something too, her too."

The owner of the hotel, who did not understand their haste, feeling guilty asked, "How can I help you?"

"Everything was marvelous," Toni said, "but we are in a great hurry. City folk always hurry."

"I deeply regret it," said the hotel owner in a voice belonging to days gone by.

"Are the horses ready?" asked Toni, distractedly.

"Ready and raring to go," said the porter with the voice of a professional servant.

Toni handed him the bank note and the porter's face blushed with shame.

Once again they were on a plain. The August light dripped from the skies, thick and hot. Toni took off her sweater and a sigh of relief burst from her. The cloud that shaded her brow had now departed, and she sat easily. Rudi was happy, too, because he had succeeded in drawing his mother out of the slough of despondency. Now only the sun and the scenery would affect her, and people would no longer muddle her thoughts. It was the same for him. Contact with the horses gave his spirit fresh air. He had longed for those dumb creatures and was happy to be in their company again.

In the afternoon they stopped near a tavern. The landlady, seeing the guests, said: "You mustn't come inside. Inside it's dirty and unpleasant. I'll bring a table outside for you, in the garden, and serve you fresh dairy dishes."

"Excellent," said Toni.

It was a provincial tavern. Toni recognized its look. It smelled bad, battered wagons stood about it, horses groaning; it was frightening.

"Home from vacation, aren't you?" said the landlady as she dragged out a wooden table and wicker chairs.

"Yes, yes." Toni's theatrical voice had returned to her. "I enjoy all this beauty around me. What a landscape!"

"What are you saying?" asked the skeptical woman. "I, at any rate, can offer you what remains of what I cooked last night, borscht and sour cream. I made it all last night. The peasants are too coarse-minded for dainty dishes. Give the peasants vodka and sausage, and you have done your duty by man and beast."

"Where are you from?" asked Toni with the local intonation.

"From here, to my regret, but I spent many years in the city."

"It's not good here?" Toni drew closer to her.

"It's a village, and all the coarseness of spirit found in villages is found here. You are Jews, are you not?"

"How do you know?" Toni was surprised.

"What do you mean? You can tell right away. I worked for Jews for many years. I know them very well."

"And you don't hate them?"

"What are you saying, Madam? The Jews are decent people, honest, they did only well by me all those years. But I, in my great stupidity, did not heed their advice and returned here. What is there here? Be so good as to tell me."

"You found nothing wrong with them?"

"No," she said, and she spoke slowly as if she were about to tell them something intimate.

"Strange," said Toni, surprised, "strange."

"You must admit that Jewish men are gracious with women. I would not trade them for those coarse fellows. They are delicate."

"Have you been back here long?"

"Many years in this den by now, serving the men vodka. For a person like me, Madam, who worked for the Jews for more than a few years and learned something from their ways, it is doubly hard."

"Aren't there any guests here?"

"Very infrequently. Who'd stop his wagon outside this den of thieves? Only drunkards or the children of drunkards."

Rudi, although he didn't understand a single word in that flow of speech, felt some closeness to the woman, whose face alternately expressed tempestuousness and grief.

"Does the young man also speak our language?" she addressed Toni.

"This is my son," Toni said. "He does not speak Ruthenian."

"Really? I was certain he was your brother. You see, one's eyes have a way of fooling one."

In the meantime a few men had gathered in the doorway of the tavern and started shouting. It was over some insult that no one was prepared to let pass. Finally it happened, it was no longer possible to prevent: a fight. Strangely, the mistress of the house did not intervene. The peasants shrank from nothing, brandishing whatever was at hand, spades and pitchforks.

"This is a daily spectacle," explained the landlady. "No need to get excited. After drunkenness comes the fight."

About an hour later the bystanders finally separated the contenders. The country doctor had his hands full. The men neither shouted nor wailed, some of them were dragged into the tavern, and others were hauled to the nearby orchard.

"Who will get me out of here?" said the landlady.

"You're still young," said Toni. "All gates are open before you."

"I have no hope. My soul yearns for the city, the shop windows and the sidewalks, for the Jews. I like Jews. I need them as I need air to breathe. The happiest hours of my life were spent in their homes. You understand?"

"And I came to seek peace in the country."

"No, Madam. Whoever is familiar with the country knows. Here nothing is splendid. A cow is a cow and a horse is a horse. And the people here have learned their manners from the beasts."

"And I came to seek peace in the country."

"No, Madam. Your fate is better than that. You are a Jewess, and you have no part of this stupidity. A man's head grows empty here like a pumpkin."

"You have nothing to envy in me," said Toni openly.

"I do envy you, Madam. The Jews have not made life unbearable for you. They have manners even in bed, pardon me. Remain in the city. Don't leave it. The Jews aren't cruel."

Meanwhile, Rudi had given the horses fodder. They were content and lay on the ground. The sun moved steadily southward, and on the crests of the nearby mountains the light in the treetops turned blue.

"Too bad you're leaving me. You brought my lost youth back from far away, and soon the nightly drunkards will arrive. What do I have in common with them?"

"Surely we'll meet again." Tears stood in Toni's eyes.

She handed the woman a bank note, which she resolutely refused to take. "What's the matter with you, Toni?" She addressed her familiarly. "You gave me back the taste of my youth."

But Toni was possessed by a strange spirit, and she said, "I must pay. No one will serve me for free."

"But that is my way of making a gift to people I like," the woman pleaded. "Who knows when I'll see you again?"

"These fields restore my spirit. When you come down to it, I was born in this territory, and I breathed this air. I brought no joy to my parents." That was her melancholy: longings, fears, cajolery. All in a single bundle. But there was no denying he loved her muddle-headedness.

The fields were spread out across the plains and mowed bare. Only the green crests of the mountains shaded them with their leafy canopy; they alone seemed to give off something of their green darkness. "What did you think of that Ruthenian woman?" Rudi asked.

"They are marvelous, I must admit. They have a kind of utter freedom. You noticed."

"But why is she dissatisfied?"

"Pay no mind. They're splendid. I love them. True, the Jews mixed them up a little, spoiled them a little, but in a year or two they will forget the Jews. That's only their way of talking."

"Isn't there a contradiction here?"

"No."

Rudi felt strength in his mother's voice.

That conversation evoked in his heart, with flaming clarity, the secret days of his childhood. The maids. They would change every month. Some were thin and nasty or fat and strict, but not one was pleasant. Foolish girls from the villages or corrupted ones from the city who would entertain their lovers in the darkened bedroom, and others who would revile their husbands in harsh and vulgar language.

He only saw his mother early in the morning between one dawning glimmer and another, but that peek was enough for him to absorb the graceful lines of her face, or rather the thin, somewhat transparent shadings that hovered over her eyes. She would immediately disappear into the obscurity of the morning. Afterward the day would seem dark, painfully sleepy, pointless.

"Where is Mommy?" his voice would sometimes cry out from within him. "She'll be back in the evening," the jarring answer would come. He learned to distract himself, to forget himself, to count coarse beads on an abacus and to amuse himself with words that he invented.

Sometimes, as if in a dream, he would see: there is no one, only he and his mother, his mother in her flowered summer dress. The thin lines of her eyebrows only made her large eyes stand out more. "This is a dream," he said to himself. Those soft strokes did not last more than a few moments, and once again there were the same fat maids whose dresses smelled of sweat and perfume, but not one speck of beauty.

"Allia is good, isn't she?" she would sometimes address him.

"Yes." What could he say that would not make her sad?

Even then he knew with the dim consciousness of a child, which is stronger than any certainly, that he would love only his mother. Any other love would be fugitive and void. Disappointments were not slow in coming, and they were bitter. She would disappear for days. "Where is my mother?" The pain would break out of him. "She'll return." He perceived an evil smile on the maid's lips.

Sometimes when she came after many days of absence, tired and changed, he would break out in tears. "It is I, your mother, an utter simpleton, but your mother who loves you." That was enough to soothe him. Those scraps of joy between twilight and twilight did not last more than a few moments, but they were sufficient to nourish the long, tortured hours that spread out like a heavy curtain of darkness.

One morning when he was five, he fell at her feet and would not release them, shouting: "Don't go." That outburst froze the astonished mother on the spot. Pleas and explanations were fruitless. Only when the mother too burst into tears did he let her go. There were also passing moments of pleasure. Like Julia. A gracious, thin servant, with whom he would sleep in the big wooden bed. She worked in their house for an entire winter. At the end of the winter his mother fired her. Apparently someone had informed on her, or she was caught stealing. Rudi, in any case, would remember her dressed in her linen frock, her face thin and dark, a smile in her eyes. Right after she left, his mother brought a big, hard woman from the suburbs, who would work and curse, sowing fear all through the rooms.

When he turned six, Toni surprised him by coming home, firing the maid, and announcing: "I myself shall prepare him for school, not a stranger." Her return, or rather the posture of her return, the armchair and the elbow, the hair scattered over the back of the chair, the shoes and the socks—all those precious details would be treasured up in his heart for many years. The preparations for school lasted a month. Toni bought him high shoes, a suit, and a sweater all at the same time, and, of course, a pencil case and notebooks. That was a marvelous summer, green-blue, with an unspotted sky.

The vacation ended. It was a large, old-fashioned school where cold, darkness, and earnestness reigned unchecked. Not even the schoolyard, surrounded by high trees, revived his heart. The teacher, a strong woman, wore a buttoned blazer and high shoes laced in front. Here for the first time all the shades of gray were revealed to him, the metallic voice, the white letters on the blackboard. Here he felt the shoves and curses. But the afternoon hours on the sofa near his mother, bundled up in a down quilt, would make his heart forget the tumult and the coarseness. Slumber would descend upon him in the form of a soft hand.

One day at recess, while he was standing in the schoolyard, a heavy blow landed on his shoulders: "Dirty Jew." It was a hard and wicked blow.

"Mommy, what's a dirty Jew?"

"Despicable words. Pay no mind."

He felt something was out of order here. Later she went on to explain: "I am actually Jewish, but not you. Your father was Christian by birth and descent, and so are you. You are not besmirched." He was happy. When they said "Dirty Jew" to him, he would answer: "Not me, maybe you." He grew tall, and Toni was pleased with his growth. She did not bother to speak at length with him unless he pestered her. They would go shopping or for a walk. The winter was short and spring came early. At that time they lived on the ground floor with a little garden outside.

When he was in the second grade a man with a long face would enter the house. Toni would make him sandwiches and coffee. It turned out he was the district physician. Toni would sit and tell him everything, all her complicated problems. He would listen and say: "Tomorrow I will write a letter. No cause for concern."

During that period she was flooded with nostalgia for her home. He would sometimes hear her voice: "The time has come to go home." At first they sounded like idle words, but in the course of time he learned: there is a distant region named Bukovina, where there are plains and woods and cattails, windmills and sawmills, and on its great river, the Prut, barges sail to the great sea. In that vast region there is a little village full of light, and its name is Dratscincz, and there his grandfather and grandmother dwell.

One day followed the next, and other unpleasant matters arose: debts and childhood diseases mingled with each other. The old doctor would come daily and treat Rudi. He himself, it turned out, was a very sick man. One day he collapsed and was not seen again. Toni wept: "He was a good man and has gone to heaven."

Afterward new months came. His love for his mother became somewhat marred. He found that her thoughts were not orderly, that she did not keep her promises, and that she sometimes concealed one detail or another. He learned to lie in wait for her, to confront her with her contradictions and predict her caprices. When he caught her in the act she would burst out laughing: "I am such a simpleton." In his youth he had already noticed that she used the word *simpleton* all the time. Years before, making a bad choice of a maid, she had announced: "A simpleton and beyond hope." As an adolescent he was very severe with his mother. He demanded order of her, and consistency, and truth. In the sixth grade his vocabulary was already larger than hers, and in his first year of high school he would inundate her with lofty speech that was beyond her grasp. "You are right," she would apologize, cornered. In her heart she was proud that her only son was intelligent, that he knew how to observe people and uncover their flaws like an experienced hunter. But as he grew older, as his thoughts became more orderly, she came to fear: "One day he will escape from me."

A simpleton and beyond hope, he was sure. There were days when he ignored her, or rather distracted himself from her as if she were an object. A feeling of superiority waxed within him as his shoulders daily grew broader. In school he was outstanding, and not only in his studies.

Toni would whisper: "He is ignoring me, and rightly so. Am I worthy of his attention?" Her heart bled, but she found not a single word to justify herself.

While everything was still suspended between one uncertainty and another, she fell into a trap once again; this time it was an elderly admirer who was less like a lover than a concerned father. He was an unreligious Czech. Years of bachelorhood had made him easygoing. He would come to their home once or twice a week and bring them two baskets full of good food. For some reason that innocent man drove Rudi wild. "Enough," he shouted, "I'm leaving home." Toni's entreaties were to no avail. "The old man is goodhearted and lonely." While their argument was at its height, the man went the way of all flesh. Two days later they received double notice: they would not be required to attend the funeral, for he had left his body to science; and he had willed his property to Toni.

In the meantime Rudi had finished the seventh grade, and his opinion of his mother had changed a bit. Perhaps because of that magic word, which the Latin teacher had used so often the previous semester: intuition. Perhaps he had discovered that she too suffered. Now, at any rate, he looked at his mother. She was prettier than all the girls with whom he passed the evenings. While they were still in doubt as to how to invest the money, a great light fell on Toni's face: "Home." Her face was always bright, but it had never had a glow like that.

Afterward, the morning was bright, full of the odor of soil and withering plants. Her heart's yearnings and fears were laid up in her face, which was a wonder. Rudi too was seized by wonder. As he stood and looked at her, he felt he was being jolted deep within. Everything he had stored up during his years at school—all the theories, the contempt for the masses and for his mother, the entrenched rampart he had fortified with his own hands—was breached. He was close to his mother as though he were near a magnifying mirror.

"Mother," he wanted to shout. Of course he did not do so. His shout turned into a question, which immediately chilled her seething heart. His mother, unexpectedly, was very clam at that time and answered to the point. She said: "I feel a strong bond to my mother and father now."

"You are no longer frightened?"

"No, darling, I feel a strong desire to do everything my parents did. I also have a strong wish for you to be Jewish."

"I am a Jew, am I not?"

"Certainly you are a Jew, but you need a few more things, not many, not difficult."

"What?"

"I wish you had a Jewish face."

"How?"

"A Jewish face is a long one. You are laughing."

"No, I am listening."

"I was an utter simpleton. I was attracted to the gentiles like a moth to the flame. An utter simpleton. It is hard for me to forgive myself. But you are a Jew in every fibre of your being. And here, in these regions, you will learn the secret easily."

"How does one learn it?"

"You shall see. The secrets are not many."

Jews did not live in Schoenburg. Once a man passed by their house, a tall man whose right shoulder was a bit stooped and whose face shone brightly. "That is a Jew," said Toni, smiling. Rudi was then seven years old, and the brightness of the man's aspect and his height remained in his memory.

Now he saw Jews for the first time but not as he had pictured them. They stood in the doorways of their low houses, their faces were neither rustic nor urban, a kind of surprise suffused their dark skin. In the little village inns they were greeted by faces glowing with hospitality. Toni spoke Yiddish to them with German words mixed in, and they listened with their mouths wide open.

These were little villages at the foot of high mountains, planted by cold streams. The birds too, he noticed, were lone birds, whose shrieks at night were sharp, as if they were about to plunge their beaks into the congealed darkness. And there were women there, of Toni's age, who greeted her warmly as a sister. Toni's hands fluttered in her great joy, and she gave away objects and goods to anyone in need.

"You should not give things away," the women advised her.

"Why not?" She was surprised. "I lack nothing, and it will do them good."

They slept late, and when they got up the table was already laden with good things to eat: black bread, sour cream and cheese.

"You feel it." Toni surprised him.

"What?"

"These are Jews."

On the sabbath the landlord took him to the synagogue. It was a wooden house of prayer, and the front windows held pictures of lions and tigers. The man showed him the letters in the front of the prayer book. The prayer book was old, and the letters had turned yellow over the many years. The old men who sat beside the Holy Ark closed their eyes. Their long, pale faces expressed quiet devotion.

After the service they crossed the park, drank water from the well, and returned to the inn. The inn was peaceful, enveloped in vines and sunk in deep sleep.

Thus they wandered from village to village. The early autumn had not yet marked the trees, which stood, shoulders thrown back and green. The yellow patches were only new thatched roofs. And in every out-of-the-way corner there were Jews. They received Toni with the warmth of surprise and joy.

Of course embarrassing questions were not lacking. But Toni endured them with an upright heart. Not she but someone else inhabited her voice. She said: "I brought my son here to see my mother's and father's faces. Perhaps he will learn some Jewishness from them. He needs it very badly." The local dialects came back to her and she spoke them with ease. In one of the villages a landlady said: "Autumn is coming. Why go far away? Stay with us. The cellar is full of good food, and there's plenty of wood for heat. The boy will study with my son, and you will rest. You need rest." He learned only afterward how right the woman had been. The familiar sights gave her much happiness, but also a hard kind of absent-mindedness. "Come, we're leaving," she would say. "We have to keep going. We won't get there in time." But of course she was prey to these sudden fears.

The autumn did come: cold and full of gray beauty. "We must travel, we must get there in time," she would urge him on, but right afterward she would regret her haste and say: "Why are you rushing? Spare me. Slow the running horses down. There is time. The grayness is not so ugly as it looks."

She was lovely, and in the peasant scarf she had bought in one of the villages her face filled with womanliness. True, even now she did not cease making vapid comments, her yearnings and scraps of memories. Once again she was not his mother, whose notions he mocked in the recessess of his heart. She was a mother with a secret in her soul. The day would soon come when that secret would burst forth and rise like a raging flame.

They were staying in the home of a widow who had lost her fortune and rented rooms to summer vacationers. The house nestled at the foot of a high mountain, on the banks of a branch of the Prut. It was a spacious home, swathed in carpets and embellished with household articles that the widow had brought back from her travels. In the living room stood a large bookcase. Toni was thrilled by the home's grace and simplicity and immediately announced: "I'm staying here."

It turned out that the woman had studied pharmaceutics in Vienna. After awhile, she and her husband had left the big city and built themselves a house here, at the foot of these mountains. "Are you religious?" Toni asked her suddenly.

"No," said the woman. "I am a Jewess, and I do not hide that from anyone, but I am not religious. And you?"

"I believe in the God of my fathers."

A soft smile rose on the woman's face and she said: "I, to my sorrow, come from an assimilated home. My late husband, too. In recent years I have felt a strong attraction for the soil of my homeland, for my parents, and for their beliefs, and now I am going home."

"Exactly. I am taking my son with me. His father was not one of our people. It is important to me for my son to be Jewish. That's funny, isn't it?" Toni said and tittered.

"We had no children," said the widow. "But I understand

what you are talking about very well. And what is his impression?"

"To my surprise it is good. He even went to synagogue. He showed no distaste."

They would stroll for hours along the river and on their return in the evening the table would be laden with cheese and sour cream, garden vegetables, the fruits of the earth. Toni no longer spoke at length, nor did she inquire. For hours she would sit in the living room and watch the river. Rudi sat and read. Once he had loved to read Karl May. Now he read whatever was at hand. Suddenly he discovered Rilke. Strange, he had first heard Rilke's name from his mother. Someone, apparently, had whispered it to her. He had not yet known then that her learning was sparse and jumbled. He had still believed that a person who had not finished school was not worthy of being called cultured. Since then two years had passed. In those two years he had learned something from personal experience. His mother had also taught him a lesson or two.

"Mother, what are you thinking about?"

"I am not thinking. I'm trying to picture grandfather and grandmother's house."

"And do you see it?"

"Strange, all those years I saw it in the minutest detail, and now I cannot visualize it." A different light dwelt in her eyes, as if she wished to glean the secret not with her mind but rather with her face and the skin of her hands.

At night before going to sleep, out of the blue, she said, "I love the cattails that grow on the banks of the Prut. They are strong cattails."

"And the trees?" Rudi asked in surprise.

"The cattails are prettier."

The next day Toni got up and said: "Enough, we are leaving." The sky was gray and the waves on the river swelled up darkly in the valley. When Toni informed the woman she intended to set out, the widow lay her hands on the table and said: "The clouds outside do not augur well. Why not stay here for another day or two until the storm has passed?" But Toni's mind was made up. "We must go, we must be there in time."

By afternoon the carriage was already prepared, the horses harnessed. "We will make every effort," Toni raised her voice, as if she were speaking from far off.

"Do you have umbrellas?"

"We have no umbrellas, but we have raincoats."

And with that haste they parted. He thought that along the way she would calm down, forget, and perhaps fall asleep. The wind was strong, a northwest wind breathing of winter. To their good fortune the road was paved, the horses were well fed, the bends in the road were few, and they progressed with no impediments. Toward evening heavy rain fell, and Rudi suggested they go to a farm to warm up.

"What are you talking about? We're late, but if you wish, we can stop here," she said, showing a strange discontent.

Luckily they had pulled up near a tavern. It was a Christian inn steeped in the odor of vodka and tobacco, almost suffocating. When Toni asked whether there was a room for the night, the landlady chuckled and said, "This is no hotel, it's a tavern. People don't sleep here, they drink." She herself was drunk. Her eyes were bleary and red.

"I told you. Let's leave this place," Toni said in a surprisingly loud voice.

"The place doesn't please you?" said the drunken lady. "What doesn't please you?"

"We are soaked, tired, and hungry. We are looking for a room to lay our heads. Is that not clear?"

"We're wet too," a peasant raised his arm, "but we don't make a fuss about it." One of the peasants shouted: "Dirty Jews."

"Let's get out of here," she said and pushed Rudi out. Rudi was stunned by the force of her shove.

When the dawn broke he saw that her face was veiled with fog, the blue in her lovely eyes had melted, an angry flash of green shot out of them. "I would love a cup of coffee," she said, as if there were no one else in the world besides her. And Rudi, who did not catch all the egotism that was inherent in that sentence, said: "In a little while. Surely we will come to an inn soon."

Afterward Toni sank into a black mood and didn't utter a word. The clouds scattered and a blue sun glowed in the sky. The wind abated and the scent of plants washed by the rain filled the air. "Mother, don't you feel well?" He gathered a few words and offered them to his mother.

"I don't know what happened to me. The whole matter seems pointless. If this is what the region looks like, I don't know what else is in store for us."

Two hours later they reached an inn. It turned out to belong to religious Jews. Toni refused to enter. "Religious people won't accept me." But thirst changed her mind, and she assented. To her surprise the inn was empty. A few tables stood covered with white rustic cloths. The fragrance of morning coffee hung in the air. "Could we have a cup of coffee?" Toni asked apologetically. "We've had nothing to eat or drink for many hours."

"My daughter, do sit down." The landlady addressed her with a gentle voice. "And meanwhile I'll prepare breakfast for you. Thank God I have enough for you."

"Are we disturbing you?" Toni asked.

"My daughter, your eyes see that there is no one here, and

that I have, thank God, good food in the kitchen. The stove is lit."

A few minutes passed and the old woman appeared with a tray full of good things to eat. Perhaps because of the tables standing in the corner, covered with white cloths, the silence reminded them of those little wayside chapels that a person can enter for a moment to take some peace of mind. For a long time they sat without talking. Toni's face kept changing expression. No strangeness was discernible in it. From time to time she made a comment or expressed wonder.

"You aren't sorry?" she addressed Rudi.

"No, Mother, why should I be sorry?"

"Why did I drag you to such remote places?"

"It's pretty here."

Suddenly it was as if a distant voice took hold of her. She got to her feet and said: "We wish to pay."

"Mother, no one is home, no one can hear you."

"Then we shall go to the window and shout. Perhaps they'll hear us."

The old woman appeared in the doorway and said: "Why are you rushing off, children?"

"We must get there, grandma, we're late."

"You've eaten nothing."

"We have eaten."

"And the boy?"

"Grandma," said Toni, "this lad is more precious to me than anything else. I brought him here to absorb some Jewishness. He doesn't know a thing. I promise you, grandma, that I will do everything to have the boy learn and know. I will not rest.

"Rudi, we must go," she called out in a voice that was not hers. She immediately took a bill out of her purse and handed it to the old woman.

"I don't know if I shall see you here again, children. Bless you, children. God preserve you."

The clouds had scattered, and on the horizon a green spot showed. The pure autumn sun stood in the firmament and shed its warmth. The winds died down.

"You will forget me," she suddenly addressed him without warning.

"What are you saying, Mother?"

"You will have other interests, and you will forget me."

"You're my mother, and I won't forget you." The words left his mouth the way he would say them when he was a child.

"I'm very frightened. I too forgot my mother."

"But we'll always be together."

"Thank you. I'm very happy I brought you home. You'll feel good here. Pay no heed to the bad things. It's a beautiful country, a broad one, and the cattails grow here like flowers. The light here is also precious." And without finishing she shut her eyes and fell asleep.

CHAPTER TWO

The end of October was chilly and damp, and no sun was seen in the sky. They passed from forest to forest without stopping. "Where are we?" Toni would rouse herself and ask from time to time. "Wake me up in the evening," and immediately she would drop her head back onto the seat. At intervals they would stop at a barn or a stand, buy potatoes, and go on their way.

The thought that everybody was sitting now, crammed into dark classrooms, studying, while he was free, with two young horses at his command, dwelled within him as a long-lasting pleasure. True, his mother could be difficult, but over time he learned that you had to talk to her calmly, make promises to her and soothe her—and, when necessary, flatter her. When you flattered her, the will to live returned to her face.

Sometimes she would wake up and say, "What are we doing here?"

"We're on a journey, Mother. Doesn't this landscape inspire you?"

"What landscape are you talking about? The humidity is eating me up."

By the beginning of November the roads were swamped with mud, his mother's head was spinning, and the horses were tired. "We have to stop somewhere," he said, and his mother agreed with him. But where could they stop? They were in the deepest heart of the hill country, cut off from every town, woods to their right and woods to their left. Here and there a cabin or abandoned hut.

"A cup of coffee, darling. Isn't there, in this whole wide world, a single cup of coffee?"

"Not far," he said, to distract her.

"No matter, we'll do without."

The tired carriage was still rocking aimlessly when houses appeared on the horizon. In recent days Rudi had lost his sense of direction, and his mother no longer cared. Just to get to a house and drink a cup of coffee.

"Let's hope this town is a merciful one," her voice trembled, "and they won't begrudge us a cup of coffee."

As they approached, it appeared somewhat different. A few low houses surrounded by high oaks. The meager structures merely emphasized the spreading power of the woods: a web of branches, leaves, and twigs.

"Where are we?" Toni's head emerged from within her coat.

"In Buszwyn, Madam," the woman answered bashfully.

"And where is the inn, Madam?"

"Nearby, Madam, nearby."

Toni's face lit up. It was as if the depressions and humiliations were suddenly wiped clean from her heart. The young light he loved so much came back and enveloped her face.

The inn turned out to be a wooden hostel run by a mother and daughter at the crossroads.

"Whence and whither in this cold?" asked the woman in quaint Yiddish.

"Homeward, grandma. The time has come to go home, hasn't it?"

"If only my daughters would say so."

"Where are your daughters?"

"In Vienna, cursed Vienna."

Immediately coffee, rolls, butter, and cheese were served. "God almighty," proclaimed Toni, "how good it is we reached this tidy house."

"How were the roads?" asked the woman, proffering some homemade plum jam.

"It's good to return home and be with people one is close to."

"You haven't seen your mother for many years?"

"Many."

"You are doing a very good deed," said the landlady, withdrawing.

The daughter showed them their room, not a spacious one, but clean and heated. The front window looked out on the forest, and the rear one was clogged with vines. There were two old wooden beds, a dresser and a writing table. Toni noticed the young woman was neat but bitter.

As in old times his mother hurried to change her clothes, made herself up, and, with a light motion, as if by the seashore, she said, "We must go out while it is still light." The view was breathtaking in its simplicity: a few houses wrapped in trees and red vines, a pigsty or woodshed in the courtyards. Suddenly a peasant and his horse appeared, as if the woods had engulfed him in their shade and hunted him down.

"Ice cream, I feel like ice cream," Toni said greedily.

"In the fall, in a place like this?" Rudi wondered.

"You're right, why did it occur to me?"

"You forgot," he tried to soften the blow.

"I always forget, don't be angry with me."

Could he be angry with her? She never scolded him, never nagged him, and she refused him nothing he wanted. If anything, she went too far. She would secretly sell her jewels to buy him boots of fine, thin leather, riding breeches, and all the accouterments of gilded youth. She wanted her son to be known not only for his talents but also for his handsome appearance, at the height of fashion, like the son of wealthy parents, if possible. His looks were truly impressive. By his second year of high school he was already going out in society, first to balls in the local dancehall, later to an inn in the suburbs, and finally to rich people's homes. He would come home late, reeking of beer. But Toni was proud. The thought that girls were competing for him gave her a feeling of spiteful pleasure. She cherished his outings. In time that little pleasure became oppressive: he loves everybody but me.

Rudi, giddy with his successes, paid no heed to those little anxieties. At the time she was merely an auxiliary to his whims, nothing more. There was no lack of nasty rumors, but they hadn't the power to darken the young man's horizons. His studies suffered, as they say, and his midterm report card no longer glowed with "Excellents." But he remained a good student.

"You're so immersed in your own diversions, you didn't notice that I haven't left the house for two days now."

"Sorry, Mother."

"You return from your *diversions* completely mixed up." There was something irritating, or rather bitter, in the way she pronounced that word.

Rudi was a smashing success, though. One evening, while the ball was at its height, a boy turned on him and hit him in the face. Rudi moved to respond, but the other, in his rage, brought the shame out into the open: Jew! Rudi looked around.

He sought help not against the attacker, but against his calumny. Strangely, no one came to his assistance.

Rudi gritted his teeth and abandoned the diversions.

It was as if that had happened years ago. Now they were standing in a dairy, devouring ice cream. It was homemade ice cream, and the taste of fresh milk flooded each mouthful. Toni was pleased, and her pleasure was clearly expressed. Her eyes glistened.

They gobbled up two big portions. She was about to order a third, but at the last minute changed her mind.

"Whence and whither?" asked the proprietor in the language of the village.

"Homeward bound. The time has come to go home, hasn't it?"

"And where is that home?"

"Not far. Two hundred miles at most. But now we're giving ourselves a little treat, an extra portion of ice cream. I must say it's splendid. You won't find ice cream like that in the city."

"Thank you," said the proprietor, and his white face blushed pink with embarrassment.

They went for a walk. They soon discovered that a river cut through Buszwyn with a stone bridge linking the two banks. On the opposite bank there were a few buildings draped in vines, and the courtyards and entrances to the homes were bathed in calm.

"Wouldn't you like to live here?" Toni surprised him. "Believe me, it's balm to the soul. You get up in the morning and light the oven, a garden next to the house, a cow in the barn. What more does one need?" Rudi noticed she was speaking a different German, a soft German.

The view was truly splendid in its tranquility. In the court-

yards men were sawing firewood, piling the logs against the
walls. Women were putting up storm windows. A peasant was
putting new shingles on his roof. Winter was still far off, but
its odor was already in the air. Rudi reflected on the coming
day of frost: the snow would pile up on all sides. No one went
in or out; inside the furnace roared. You'd wrap yourself up in
a blanket and read a book.

The rumor flew: a beautiful woman had arrived from Austria with her son. When they returned from their walk, the
guests of the inn were already waiting to view the marvel with
their own eyes. Toni was in an ebullient mood. She drank
coffee and devoured two cheese cakes. "She's lovely," the
comment buzzed about the room.

Later they brought in the gramophone and everyone danced
waltzes until late in the evening. Rudi was overcome with
fatigue. The sights of the day flooded him and numbed his
senses. He collapsed fully dressed on his bed like a sack.

The next day the light at the window was full and unstained. But Toni's face was washed out, as if some inner tur-
moil had taken its toll on her. "What happened to me? What
evil have I done?" she asked bitterly as she sat in her bed.
Rudi recognized that voice. A mixture of oppression and foolishness. That was how she used to sound when she came home
after a humiliation or an abject failure.

"Nothing, it just seems that way to you," Rudi said distractedly.

"I'm mixed up," she said, burying her face in the pillow.

This time it turned out there was no confusion. Her face
was burning, and her whole body was shaking. The doctor
who came in the afternoon pronounced without hesitation,
"You must stay in bed."

At night her delirium grew, and she spoke unceasingly, a
welter of words: the present, the past, the scoundrels, and the

generous souls. There was no anger in her delirium. It was as if she wished to be reconciled with everyone. She was thirsty, and Rudi brought her a glass of water.

"You love me," she returned the empty glass.

"Of course I love you, Mother."

"Now I don't care about anything." Her head sank on the pillow.

In the morning it was already clear: typhus. The rumor quickly spread and terrified the place out of its tranquility. The innkeeper wrung her hands and said, "What do they want of that woman?" The two servant men came and made her face reality. On a flat stretcher, unceremoniously, like two cold gravediggers, they took her straight to the quarantine room of the infirmary.

The doctor, an elderly man with a calm expression, quietly explained that from now on his mother had to be in complete isolation. "And I?" asked Rudi. He immediately corrected himself: "What must I do?"

"Nothing, only wait. Nurse Maya and I will take care of her."

He asked no more. For a long time he stood stock still, without uttering a word. Then he went to the dairy and ate two portions of ice cream. The cold ice cream inebriated his senses. He felt weak, fatigued.

Her fever rose daily. The doctor came twice a day to take her temperature and give her medicine. Through the screened window Rudi could see her pale face resting weakly on the pillow.

"How is my mother?" he would cautiously ask the doctor.

"With God's help she'll get better." The doctor's look expressed a kind of frightening religiosity.

He would stand next to the window for hours and follow every shadow tensely. That tension brought visions of past

days to his eyes. Not particularly heartening visions, like the
football field where he used to spend hours. They played wild
games. The boys would shove, hit, and kick mercilessly. There,
with relentless devotion, he defended his secret Jewishness
like a defect one doesn't know the meaning of. Sometimes his
mother would appear with Prince Konicz and withdraw him
from that fervor.

Toni had fallen in love with Prince Konicz when Rudi was
in the eighth grade. He was a man of the noblest blood who
had lost his family connections as well as his fortune and sup-
ported himself with the two ancient castles his parents had
bequeathed him. He lived in a modest apartment outside the
city near the workers' quarter. His noble forefathers had left
him but one minor passion, the desire to collect paintings. He
never overcame that weakness. It was apparently from him
that Toni had learned the names of a few well-known artists,
authors, and musicians. He presented her with two drawings
by Ludwig Mayer, but Toni did not know their value.

In the evening Rudi would sit for hours waiting for her to
return. Very angry, he would fall asleep on the sofa. At that
time he stored up a lot of anger. He practiced to preserve that
anger forever. She apparently divined his intention and tried
to mollify him. When she returned at night she would spread
a blanket on the floor and sleep near him. Sometimes when
he awoke he would see her curled up at his side, her being
reduced to that of a sleeping child.

Now he stood outside and tried to forgive her for everything. It was important to him that she also forgive him for
the sins he had committed against her, and there were more
than a few: ignoring her, arrogance, the outbursts when he
had called her hopelessly rash. True, he had never called her
an idiot, but deep inside he had been certain she was an utter
fool. True, as the days passed other thoughts about his mother

also arose within him, but he kept them to himself and never revealed them to anyone.

"How do you feel, Mother?" he would cry out.

She seemed to have heard his call, but she didn't have the strength to open her eyes.

The next day the district health officer came. He seemed younger than the local doctor, and was meticulously dressed. It was evident that the visitor regarded the doctor with contempt. He spoke without looking at him. He was concerned with the quarantine more than with the patient. At the door he said: "She must be totally isolated, you hear?" He immediately got in his coach and disappeared from the town.

"Will my mother be herself again?" Rudi asked, not knowing what to do.

"God who heals the sick will heal your mother."

Afterward the doctor invited Rudi to the dairy. They drank coffee and ate poppy cakes. The doctor's face expressed great wonderment. As if he were not a doctor who had seen many deaths in his life, but a man thinking mysterious thoughts.

"Where were you heading?" he asked.

"My mother," said Rudi with a serious voice, "became fed up with city life and decided to return home."

"How long have you been on your way?"

"Three months already. Mother was very happy to be going home. But now what will we do?"

"No need to worry, my dear friend. You'll soon be on your way again."

"Thank you," said Rudi.

"Don't thank me," said the doctor, "only the will of God."

Sitting so long by the infirmary dulled his dread. He would sit for hours without moving. From time to time he peeked through the window. He would spend the afternoons in the dairy, devouring ice cream and cake. Eating hungrily among passers-by, strangers, village girls, and peasants amused him a bit. In the evening he would return to the inn tired as if after an exhausting day.

In the inn a few ill-intentioned faces lay in wait for him, interested in Toni's fate. They were, it turned out, Jewish sales agents who traded in wood and grain. Not infrequently they would forget they had wives and children in another town. Rudi noticed that they wore striped blue suits, smoked cigars, and spoke to each other in a language part German, part Yiddish, and part Ruthenian. They addressed him in German, frighteningly practical.

He seldom met with the doctor. The combination of medical science and faith threw him off. The doctor's religious tones would infect him with melancholy. In his soul he prayed for his mother's recovery, but it was a wordless prayer, completely out of view.

"Do you observe the tradition?" asked the doctor.

"No," answered Rudi. "We are freethinkers." As he said it, it was as if his fear vanished, a strength, or rather an anger, filled him. "I will protect my mother with all my might."

But in the meantime he himself fell into the trap: a Ruthenian servant, a pretty well-built girl who brought the morning coffee to his room.

"How is your mother?" she surprised him.

"Better." He was astonished by the German words that had left her lips. "Where did you learn German?"

"I worked in the city for a year, for Jews, and I learned there."

"Wasn't it hard for you?"

"No. It was very pleasant," she said, baring a strand of pearly teeth.

Girls like her studied at his school. He remembered them now very clearly, especially Zawda, a well-developed girl with an opaque smile. Every time she was called to the blackboard she would burst into tears. Numbers made her dizzy, she said. Her father, a landowner, would be summoned to the head-master monthly. He was like his daughter, strongly built and of average height. A smell of pastures arose from his thick clothing. Once he slapped Zawda's face in the hallway. It seemed to be a powerful slap. It was heard in all the class-rooms.

Were it not for the wealthy father, she would have been expelled by high school. The studies were too hard for her, as simple as that. In the second year the teachers no longer ad-dressed questions to her. She would sit in the first row, staring; she was preoccupied with her own development, already ma-ture, like a woman.

Occasionally, to amuse the class a little, the mathematics teacher would suddenly call on her. She would become terri-fied, turn white, and burst into tears. But mostly the teachers didn't disturb her. At the end of the second year the third year boys fell on her and raped her in the park.

A great fuss was made. They brought in the police, the head of the city council, and several of the elderly school trustees. Finally her father was called in. He appeared in a dark, striped suit, his funeral uniform.

At the end of the day the storm subsided. Zawda's father left the headmaster's office, and, without a word, grabbed his daughter and beat her black and blue. Afterward she no longer showed herself. For a few weeks people still talked about her; but in time her name became an insult. Fathers belabored their daughters with it, and teachers, the slower pupils.

That had all taken place but two years ago. Now it seemed just a faint memory. In a few short months he had been taken far away from himself and his life. Now his mother too had removed herself from him.

The next day when the maid appeared with the coffee tray he asked, "What do you plan to do?"

"Nothing," she said with charm and self-deprecation.

"You wouldn't want to go back to the city?"

"I don't know." As she spoke her teeth showed.

He didn't have to pull her into bed.

"What's your name?" he asked her after they were finished.

"Tenya."

Most of the day he stood near the screened window trying to exchange a look with Toni. Toni had a high fever, and the words that escaped her lips expressed painful dread. As for him, his feelings were growing duller. His mother's ravaged face no longer affected him. He thought about Tenya. She wore tight blouses and perfumed her neck with cheap scent.

"My mother is sick, and I'm fornicating." Sometimes a guilty thought would pass through his mind.

But he also blamed her for being impulsive, for abandoning him on winter nights. Princes meant more to her than her son. Only the sight of the doctor's anguished face, his devotion, would suddenly flood him with a strong feeling of revulsion for his own body. Ultimately it was a passing revulsion. He spent more and more time with Tenya. She made love like an animal, with utter abandon.

That simple girl was not quite so simple. She had her own ideas, calculations. "You'll be going away soon, and what will become of me? People will wag their tongues about me." He knew it was just a pretense, a demand for compensation. And he was quite generous: once perfume, once a silk shawl. Those presents gave them both the pleasure of self-deception.

The inn was not lacking for strange sights: the landlady's young son, born in her middle age, would sit for hours in the dining room and torture himself with algebra problems. He was preparing for the entrance examinations to the *gymnasium*. His nervousness utterly confused him. "He is very able, but he has a little trouble with mathematics. He knows his history. You can test him," his mother would try to sweeten the bitter pill of her shame.

The boy's forehead was covered by messy bangs, and his face always expressed a strange effort. He would spend the day eating and solving mathematics problems. His excessive eating did not seem to help his studies. He grew fatter, and his movement became clumsier from day to day.

"How is your mother?" The landlady embarrassed Rudi again.

"Better," he said, distractedly.

"You have nothing more to worry about," she said. She knew what Rudi was doing in the mornings in his room, but as an experienced innkeeper, she knew one should pass over bedroom matters in silence. But she was strict with Tenya. "You're getting lazy about cleaning the rooms."

As the frost increased daily, Toni awakened from her illness and said, "Rudi," The doctor's happiness knew no bounds. "Rudi," she whispered again, ignoring her savior, who never moved from her bedside. She immediately closed her eyes again.

"Thank you very much," Rudi hurried over to the doctor.

"You must not thank me, my boy, only God the gracious and all-merciful."

Rudi stood like a vessel full of shame, and, involuntarily, he said, "You're right." But in his heart he was angry at the doctor for forcing him to agree.

Afterward cold, damp days came. The agents and traveling salesmen would sit in the dining room for hours after dinner and tell old jokes. From time to time a peasant would burst in and threateningly demand money or property. The agents would immediately go over to him and cajole him until he calmed down and left contented. In the evening everyone would assemble, men and women together, and play poker. The cold winds fanned the passions of the game. At the end of the night the losers would be in low spirits, the winners gay. The landlady couldn't manage to keep her youngest son away from the gaming. He was banished to his room, but there was a hole in the wall that gave him a good view.

Rudi spent his mornings with Tenya. That pleasure brought no ease to his senses. He would go to the infirmary despondent like a peasant who had wasted a month's wages in a tavern. One morning Tenya told him she had a fiancé in her village. The confession angered him, and he said, "Why didn't you tell me?"

"What is there to tell?" she said. A warmhearted and cunning smile spread across her face.

He was embarrassed: he had betrayed his own vanity.

The next day Toni opened her eyes wide: "A cup of coffee." The doctor bent his head and doffed his hat like a believing peasant who has heard a hidden voice.

"Where are we?" asked Toni.

"In Buszwyn, Upper Buszwyn," the doctor spoke to her loudly.

"I understand," Toni said weakly.

"I am the doctor, and this is nurse Maya," he introduced her.

"Did you eat?" Why didn't you eat?" she spoke to Rudi and ignored the doctor's presence.

"I ate, Mother."

"Excuse me," Toni said and closed her eyes.

The doctor's joy knew no bounds.

Afterward they sat in the buffet and drank coffee. He had been tied down to this out-of-the-way place for years now, because of his divorced wife, who had settled in this swamp to spite him. The children were no better than their mother. But what could he do? Could he leave them and emigrate to America? Rudi saw clearly that the man was lost.

"I do not love the provinces in my heart. Nature seems to make one stupid," said the doctor.

"Is the city better?"

"I don't know whether it's better, perhaps it too is corrupt."

"Where is our proper place then?"

"In faith."

He had never heard such a remark pass the lips of someone who had graduated from a university. In school only the priest discussed matters of faith. Another surprise: Doctor Laufer did not refer to the Jewish faith, but the the Russian Orthodox church. A few years ago he had converted because that was Dostoyevski's religion. As soon as he mentioned Dostoyevski's name his face lit up.

The next day Toni woke up and didn't ask where she was. She knew she was in Buszwyn. She remembered the inn, the proprietress, and she recalled the two servants who had carried her on the stretcher.

"What have you been doing?" she asked with a strangely surprised tone.

"Nothing," he lied brazenly.

"You look well. Why was I worried?"

Her face had grown very thin, and on her pale, bare throat a blue vein throbbed. But the will to live already glowed in her eyes. The doctor's prognosis—that from now on her hunger would be boundless—was completely borne out. She greedily devoured whatever was in reach.

"What's your name?" she asked the nurse.

"My name is Maya," the woman answered in a soft voice.

"What a pretty name. Your parents loved you, didn't they?"

"I grew up in a foundling home, Madam, and they gave me the name there."

"You're a free woman, then."

At those words Maya chuckled, and all her heavy limbs laughed with her.

The next day Rudi was given permission to go in. Toni lay propped up on pillows, and her thin face expressed youthful surprise. He was thrilled by that freshness and felt unclean.

"Look what I've gone and done," she said, the way she would after doing something foolish.

"It doesn't matter, Mother. There's time."

"What are you talking about? Winter is liable to come early, and we'll be stuck here." Her voice was pure, as if the words had been burnished in the fever of her illness.

He soon saw that her head was full of plans and wishes. Everything that had been stored up during her illness now poured out.

As usual, clothing. "I would like a new dress. Where can one buy a new dress here? Winter is coming, and I don't have a warm dress."

At the inn they greeted Toni with shouts of joy. The clerks and agents filled her room with gifts: boxes of candy and perfume. Toni was moved by their welcome. Her emaciation gave her face a new kind of beauty.

Tenya vanished. She took her final wages and never returned.

"Where is Tenya?" asked a clerk, an admirer of hers. "Don't ask," said the proprietress. "You'd do better asking the river why it overflowed than to ask a village girl."

Meanwhile winter descended upon them. The yard, which had been swamped in mud for the previous few weeks, was covered with snow. All at once the snow erased the yellow stains that had made the place ugly and smelly. A thick white curtain stretched to the edge of the forest.

While the snow was falling Rudi remembered the horses. He hadn't seen them for weeks. His forgetfulness frightened him into action, and he cried, "Where is the stableman?" The landlady's youngest son, who was sitting in the dining room with his yellow notebooks, was startled. "What's the matter?"

His fear was not in vain. The horses had been left in the stable with no one to watch over them. He was enraged. He called the stableman a good-for-nothing rogue, and he was about to beat his helper. The days of confusion and tension had marked him, too. He was tired, wrung out, and the emaciated horses, shivering beside the open door, kindled his wrath. "In the end we ignore what is dearest to us," the thought pierced his head.

Toni returned to normal. Except in the way she ate. She simply gobbled down her food.

"Mother, why are you eating so fast?" he couldn't help commenting.

"Sorry, I'm hungry."

Daily the sky grew darker, and setting out became unthinkable. Rudi no longer trusted the stableman. He prepared the fodder for his horses with his own hands, he watered and groomed them. Quiet contact with the dumb animals restored his sense of proportion—or rather, it restored the way he liked to look at the world and at his mother: from a distance. But in the meantime Toni spread joy and laughter about her. Even the landlady's bitter daughter, who constantly nagged and shot poisoned barbs at the servant girls, was forced to admit that Toni was a special kind of woman. Not to mention the clerks and agents. They went out of their minds. They vied with each other: who was wittier, more brilliant? Outside, every day brought a new snowstorm. The place closed in on itself. No one came or went. The landlady stood at the door of her inn as if to announce: as long as we have wood in the shed and potatoes in the cellar, I'm not worried. On the contrary. Let it snow. I love those white flakes.

Two weeks after her recovery, memories began to flood Toni. She remembered Prince Konicz and another prince whose name Rudi had heard from the maid. Toni spoke of them as if they were distant creatures, cut off from life and sunk in dark regions. She ceased speaking of her father and mother, as if they had vanished from her horizon. Eventually her memories led her to a kind of practical conclusion: "How good it is not to depend on anyone, that I need no favors." Strange, she never mentioned the man who had done the most for her by leaving her his estate, not a single word. "Strange," Rudi said to himself. "We have no gratitude for our true benefactors."

Every once in a while, as if to disrupt the calm with terror, evil tidings would filter through to them, imposing a moment of disquiet on the warm dining room. Of course it was peddlers whom the snow bore on its shoulders and brought there. Who believes peddlers? They always imagine frightful things. Give your mind over to the beauty of the snow and not to the bad news, proclaimed the landlady. So long as the snow is master of all, nothing bad can befall us. The landlady had her own reckonings. This year the winter had been good to her. The clerks and agents were unable to leave the region. The place was full to capacity. She had to entertain them, to feed them, to promise them: you won't ever forget this winter.

The activity drove her to distraction. She forgot her daughters, everything that had happened to her in that isolated place in the course of the years, the daughter who was consumed with melancholy, the son of her old age. She was pleased with the huge income the winter had brought her. That forgetfulness took away the last bit of her charm. Her eyes gleamed with avarice.

Toni's looks returned to her, and she seemed younger than her years. Everyone courted her shamelessly. "Where's Toni?" "Did you see Toni?" "She's behaving like the Princess of Rotenburg," the landlady's daughter grumbled silently.

Tenya did not return. Before she left he had given her a gold bracelet that Toni had received from Prince Konicz. It was an antique Venetian bracelet set with little diamonds that Toni wore on rare occasions.

"Do you like it?" he asked.

"Yes."

"Then it's yours."

Of course Tenya didn't ask where it came from or how he'd gotten it. The jewelry suited her wrist. "Mother has enough jewels," the evil thought flitted through his mind. Tenya did not return. Apparently her fiancé had grasped the nature of the jewelry and didn't let her come back. Rudi had no regrets. But now, seeing his mother seated at the table, her left arm bare, he was angry with himself.

The doctor announced, "There are no signs of the illness left. You must rest. The winter is good for resting." His anxious face expressed hidden joy. Strange, he didn't speak about his Russian Orthodox faith, but about Dostoyevski, the wisest of all men.

Toni handed him a bundle of bank notes and said, "Thank you."

"I won't take it," he said with a scattered movement, as if he'd been served carrion.

"We give it to you, and you may do what you wish with this lucre. You know just who needs it."

"Why did she say lucre?" Rudi wondered.

"*I* certainly don't, in any case," he was somewhat appeased.

"Of course. You will give it away, you'll distribute it."

"Do you have enough? The winter will be long."

"I do, thank God. God was generous to me this year." Toni put the money in an envelope, as if to hide its impurity from him. "It isn't as much as it seems," she said. The doctor took the money and said, "We'll go out," using the first-person plural for some reason.

"It's snowing. Why not eat with us?" said Toni in a motherly voice.

"Patients are waiting for me. Typhus is raging in the villages again. I have only two quarantine rooms. The stupid peasants are worse than beasts." As he said it, he realized he had sinned with his lips. He immediately took up his medical case and, without saying goodbye, as if escaping, he turned to the door.

A change took place in his mother's eyes, he noticed. Also a slight change in the posture of her neck, in the way she listened to him; her distraction seemed to have abated. Several times she said, "What do you think?" as if to test him. The change was somewhat disquieting to him. He was used to testing, not being tested.

During this time evenings at the inn were merry. They played cards until late, rummy, bridge, and poker. They drank coffee and smoked. Toni, of course, was the center of it all. Her beauty had not been dulled by the illness. On the contrary, it was as if several hidden lines had been revealed in her eyes. Rudi too enjoyed attention. He had grown taller, and in his new boots he looked not like a high school boy whose studies had suddenly been interrupted, but rather like a student home for Easter vacation.

"What's so bad here?" the proprietress asked one of the

traveling salesmen, who was seized with guilt feelings. The salesman, momentarily astounded by the landlady's direct question, was struck dumb. He stood next to her, tall and awkward, and finally had to admit: "It's not bad here, not bad at all. The cheese omelette is excellent."

But Rudi felt ill at ease. If it weren't for the snow, he would have harnessed the horses and taken his mother out of there. January passed like a continuous darkness. Nor did February bring any light. The meals were served on time, appetites were large. The maids worked from morning to late at night, without pause.

In February Toni was occasionally struck by fear. "Darling, what are we doing here? We're being lazy. They'll roast us in hell." She spoke freely because she knew that for once her laziness was entirely justified. The snow rioted unchecked. The roads were blocked, no one could come or go. Even the post sled ceased taking risks. The landlady's daughter would sometimes burst into the dining room and make remarks as bitter as wormwood. True, the agents and clerks were unkind to her, ignored her. Her mother's pleas were useless. "Be easy, be calm, smile." The daughter had been ill-tempered from birth, constantly dissatisfied and bitter. The passing years did not calm her. A thick wrinkle creased the breadth of her neck. When she was annoyed the wrinkle turned red and looked like a fresh scar. Rudi would look at her as if she were an abundant source of hidden secrets. She apparently was aware of it. She was sure Rudi was lying in wait to discover her hidden flaws and then mock them with the agents and clerks. She would flee from him at a run, whispering, "Here he comes, the evil one, the spirit."

Thus February passed. In March the snow began to melt, but not all at once. Cold south winds gnawed at the whiteness and left dark stains in it. There was no beauty in that disintegration, only restlessness. The clerks were seized by panic.

One of the clerks, a foolish one, imposed himself on Toni. He told her that not far from there he owned a large house, fertile land, a forest, horses. He was so enchanted with Toni's beauty that he lied to her. They all knew him, that he was just a clerk, that it was doubtful whether he had a bed of his own in his poor mother's house in the village.

Strangely, Toni didn't make fun of him. She spoke to him as one speaks to a younger brother, openly and easily. Rudi was surprised at the way she spoke to him. It occurred to him that she had once spoken that way to princes and counts. Unbeknownst to him that thought erased a certain old resentment, one whose essence he no longer remembered.

"Darling, why are you staring at me? Did I do something foolish again?"

"No."

"I'm glad. We have to prepare for our journey, right?"

"Certainly," said Rudi, and to himself he said, "She doesn't mean it seriously."

But they could no longer put off the inevitable. The winds dissolved the snows, and the dark stains changed color and became green. The clerks and agents scattered every which way as if in panic. In that commotion there was no lack of bitter and sad words, not to mention scandal. A peasant woman appeared at the door of the inn and demanded that the criminal, Attorney Sztom, be delivered to her. She was pregnant, by him and none other. Who didn't know Sztom there? The word *criminal* didn't fit him at all. Thin as a rail and expressionless. All winter long he had lain in bed and complained of indigestion. "You're looking for him? He's the one you're after?" another of the remaining agents spoke to her. She was Dunya, who gave her favors to many men. Perhaps she had gotten the name wrong. Because you couldn't imagine Sztom sleeping with a woman.

"There are good Jews and bad Jews," she stuck to her opinion. "The good ones should be protected, and the bad ones should be turned over to the police, because they're cheats." The landlady knew that over the years many of her guests had spent a night or two with her. Many of them had showered her with money and candy, and others had defrauded her and not paid a penny. When she was young Dunya had been proud that Jews came to her hut. Now that she was older, her age was speaking in her throat. She was frightened, and in her great fear she told lies. The landlady did not rebuke her to her face but spoke to her at length and in the peasant dialect. In the end she served her, as an old acquaintance, cake and a cup of coffee.

The stableman brought the horses out into the yard. The young horses, which just a few months ago had been fresh and firm, had fallen in stature. Darkness lay on their long faces. They stood motionless, as if the hunger for open spaces had been taken from them. Rudi wanted to go to them, to touch their skin and comfort them.

The stableman brought out a bucket and brush and washed the horses down. He had washed them the day before. Now he only wanted to make an impression on their owner. He brushed their bellies with all his strength. "Not so hard," Rudi wanted to tell him. The horses' passive stance saddened him, and he left.

But Toni was content and packed the suitcases diligently. A quiet joy dwelt in her face. He also noticed: she was taking care to put every object in its place, easy to reach. A kind of composure. Did it suit her, he wondered.

Toni said, "The weather is better. There are signs of spring everywhere, the horses have rested, we have a pleasant trip in store for us." The words sounded as if she were reciting a poem whose rhymes were not particularly skillful.

The landlady hugged Toni and said, "Fortune smiled upon us this winter, you adorned our house like a flower." Upon hearing those words Toni closed her eyes. The landlady's son, who was sitting on the steps, twisted his face in an idiotic expression. He, of course, would not take his entrance examinations. The German and mathematics tutor had received his severance pay and gone back to the city. "Why wear the boy out with abstractions? He'll make his way in life without all that," the tutor said arrogantly. His mother had accepted the verdict quietly, and, in the evening, in great pain, she had cried silently.

Her daughter stretched out a shrunken white hand. "It was pleasant. See you soon," she said dryly, with a bit of spiteful pleasure. She, at any rate, would not stand at the window to watch the carriage drive off. Finally the two Ruthenian chambermaids came into the room and picked up the suitcases. Toni distractedly looked over the empty room for a moment and said, "Thank you for your help." Toni knew they had only come for their tips, but she still pretended they had come to take their leave of her. "I shall remember these days with great pleasure," she said with a choked voice, and she immediately thrust money into each one's hand. They blushed in great contentment and satisfaction.

The narrow corridor, the double-glazed windows, the stairs that had resounded all winter long with energy and hope were suddenly laid bare, as if after a sudden evacuation. The landlady stood in the corner, her face in disarray, for her world had been destroyed in broad daylight. Toni hugged her very gently.

"Why are you going? Why are you leaving me?" she wailed and wept.

"I shall return, I promise," she said, although she didn't believe her own words.

CHAPTER THREE

The snows had melted, but on the peaks of the distant mountains the ice still glistened. "Pleasant, isn't it?" said Toni, wrapping her face in her woollen shawl. Water rushed in the streambeds with a deafening roar. Rudi was angry with himself. Since morning the vision of the antique bracelet he had given so offhandedly to the servant girl had not left his eyes. He knew his mother would never ask what had happened to that valuable ornament. Objects, even expensive ones, were of no account to her. She received them and gave them away without a qualm. Nevertheless he was angry for having treated his mother's jewelry with disrespect.

After an hour on the way, the intoxicating air and the odor of the horses' sweat made his anger fade. He went back to observing his mother. It was pleasant to be close to her.

In the afternoon Toni woke from her nap and said, "We're getting closer. Three or four hundred miles, no more than that. How many miles a day can we do, by your reckoning?"

"Twenty, it seems to me."

"So I assume we'll arrive in two weeks, right?" She looked at her son. A hidden dread had lurked within her since they had set out. Now it left her. Now she knew her son would not abandon her. "Rudi?" she said.

"What, Mother?"

"I want you to know: your grandfather and grandmother are observant Jews. They will certainly ask you many questions. I am sure you will know how to respond. Jews are accustomed to asking. It is not coarseness."

"She is afraid," the thought flashed through Rudi's mind.

"I would not want to make them unhappy. You understand?"

"Of course I understand."

"I would like to ease their minds."

"Obviously," he said. That word, which was meant only to express agreement with her, conjured up an old feeling in her like an evil spirit, bitter and painful, that her son mocked her in the depths of his heart, was contemptuous of her weak character and limited education. She fell silent. Rudi felt he had not behaved well. He halted the horses and said, "I plan to tell them that my identification with my mother is absolute."

"I did not ask you to go so far," she restrained her emotions.

"I am a Jew like you," he said and kissed her forehead. The horses reared up, the carriage tore off, and they sailed along.

In the long winter evenings at the inn he had observed the guests closely. At first he had not liked them. They seemed clumsy to him, ill-mannered and corrupt. But in the course of time he found that while they were not particularly pleasant, they were not unbearable. They had a sense of humor, were frivolous and extravagant. Even their complaints were just a form of humor. If that is how Jews are, why do people hate them so much?

"They have no courage," one of the clerks explained to him, a short man who played poker for hours on end.

Because of his enormous losses, he sank up to his neck in quicksand. Finally, out of pity, the other players decided to return his money. People actually did give it back—not gladly, of course.

"They don't stick to their guns, you understand?"

"How is that?" Rudi challenged him.

"The simple ability to raise their hands, to get angry without boiling over, that natural ability is denied them. That is the source of all evil: fear, cunning, pain, and self-abnegation. In short: they weren't meant for life." The explanation had no charm. A kind of unpleasant grating sound accompanied his speech. He was obviously talking about himself. Nonetheless Rudi felt there was some truth in his voice.

"A cup of coffee. I need a cup of coffee," Toni's voice of long ago returned to her.

"A little while, Mother."

"You haven't eaten or drunk either."

"I'm not hungry."

She desired his voice again. She wanted to listen to him. But Rudi, as if in spite, kept silent. His gaze was concentrated on the horses. The horses climbed up the mountain, putting their muscles to work and exhaling thick clouds of vapor.

For some reason Toni recalled her school days. Unlike her son, she had not been an excellent pupil. In the secretarial school where she had been sent she had had to stay back a year. She was fourteen then. Her parents thought her failure was a catastrophe. Who would have believed that their daughter, the darling of their soul, would fail so disgracefully? Mathematics, of course. They all took pity on her, they pleaded. The date for a second examination was even set, but the headmaster stood his ground: she must stay back. Her parents were summoned from home. In their dark clothing they looked like mourners. Toni's shame was an open wound.

Her parents could not bear the ignominy. They withdrew her from the school. A private tutor came once a week to teach her German and arithmetic. He was a tall, afflicted man who repeatedly told her how much trouble he was going to: the waiting, the train trip, the bumpy wagon ride, and in the end what does he find? A head empty of all knowledge, vacant eyes, and silent lips. Forget his troubles, what about her poor parents? All their expenses. Finally he stopped coming, for another reason. He fell ill and was sent to the mountains to recover. Toni felt a bit easier.

She worked at home and bloomed. Her beauty became famous. Her mother did not hide her apprehensions from her. "What will become of you? Everyone stares at you." Toni was not afraid. Since she had left school her life had fallen into place. She did her chores, even read a book in the afternoon to show she was not sitting idly by. Marriage proposals, of course, were not long in coming. "She's only fifteen years old," her mother said anxiously. "What do they want of me? She still has to study." That was merely a pretext. Toni did not study. She blossomed, simple as that.

To Toni's surprise her parents began to be more scrupulous about Jewish law. Her mother would get up early and pray, and her father began putting on his phylacteries in the morning again. Besides that, there was cleanliness. Now they began moving the cupboards twice a week, beating the carpets and scrubbing the front steps with white sand. Cheerful talk died out, and in its place came practical matters: "What time is it? How much money is left? Do we have firewood?" If someone came to the house and said, "Toni gets prettier every day," her parents lowered their eyes as if hearing bad tidings. At home they would recall, and not infrequently, her departed sister Gusta. Gusta had finished school with excellent grades. After her studies she had been about to marry a boy of high lineage, a young lawyer, for whom a brilliant future was predicted. But Gusta fell ill, a mortal illness protracted over two full years. The urgent trips to Vienna straitened their means. At last the poor girl died at home, because her parents no longer had the means to hospitalize her. The mother never forgave herself or her husband for not selling the house and traveling to France, where they might have found a cure for their sick daughter. The year Gusta died Toni was ten. Even then her life in school was not easy. Everyone had a favorable memory of Gusta, and they reproved Toni. Occasionally her mother would fall upon her and slap her cheek hard. Later she stopped doing that.

Toni was seventeen when she ran off with August. She did so in delusion, not in anger. When she recognized the gravity of her actions, it was too late. Return was impossible. True, she had written several long letters, sent several telegrams, but no answer came.

Then, two years ago, in an out-of-the-way cafe, she had met a not-so-young woman who was looking for work. The woman was bewildered by the strange city, and her bewilderment gave her away immediately: she was from Bukovina. It turned out she had studied in the very same secretarial school where Toni had failed. After two minutes of conversation the woman had raised her hands in surprise and said: "It's Toni!" From her, Toni had learned that her mother had been ill several years ago but had recovered, that her father was still working part-time in the sawmill. Toni was embarrassed, and in her confusion she said, "I'm in a hurry. Why don't we meet here tomorrow? Why don't we have a nice long talk? I know my way around here." She hastily handed her some money and set a date to meet there the following day. The next day she went back. She even came early, but the woman never appeared again.

That, in fact, was what had opened the crack. Since the encounter her thoughts had not stopped plaguing her. They plagued her secretly, but in clear terms: "You must return home in time. Your father and mother will forgive you." She was certain they would forgive her. Only after a time that certainty left her.

The carriage proceeded slowly. Once again she saw the woman in her mind's eye, clearly, and this time she was not panicked. A kind of surprise was written on her face, as if some wonder had seized her and would not release her.

"Rudi, isn't it strange?" Tonis said in a surprised tone.

"What?"

"To return home."

"Mother, forget your grandiose ideas for a moment. I see a grocery store."

Upon hearing those words, Toni felt a sense of relief pass over her body, as though her son had proclaimed that all her sins were forgiven now, that they had never been.

About an hour later Toni had already spread a cloth on the ground, her looks had come back to her, and she said: "Nature is truly splendid here." That was one of her clichés, for she had no words of her own. But now, for some reason, the saying suited her face. Her eyes shone, and joy flooded her—the joy that flowed within her in a kind of abundance, whose secret Rudi never understood.

They ate bread and butter and drank coffee for dessert. The soft spring light sheltered their simple meal. That good silence also pervaded the next leg of their journey that day. They passed by poor houses, chapels, and churches. Suddenly a glow in the strong greenness: a synagogue made of dark brown wood, firm in its low stature and veiled in lovely shadows.

"I was born here," Toni could no longer restrain her emotions, and she broke into speech. "I love this land. Is it a sin to love one's native land?" Her eyes clouded over with marvel like that of a believer who gives himself a moment to avow his wonderment. "If I reach home and find grandfather and grandmother in good health, I vow to change my ways."

"Mother, really," Rudi narrowed his eyes skeptically.

Her brow clouded, and all the light that but a moment ago had surrounded her forehead now went out. Rudi was about to scold her, but seeing her face swamped in melancholy he held back.

"An inn, is there no inn here?" she asked a passerby in despair.

"Two hours' journey straight ahead, there's an excellent inn," the man spoke to her softly. "An inn that will suit your taste, I'm sure. Where are you traveling?"

"Homeward."

"That is good, marvelous."

"What's good about it?" she spoke insolently.

"Nothing is better than that," the man said and left them, a smile wrinkling his lips.

Toni burst into tears.

"What happened, Mother?" Rudi stopped the horses.

"Nothing at all, my dear, I'm frightened."

"You have nothing to fear. In two hours we'll reach the inn. There we'll get fresh coffee." Rudi used whatever was at hand to quell the storm.

"Everything frightens me."

"There is nothing to fear," he said and pulled her to him tightly. He meant only to protect her, but his hug only made her weep more. "I'm stupid. I'm a sinner," she whimpered.

"The sinners are the ones who cheated you all those years," Rudi raised his voice. "They trifled with you. They did you out of your last pennies, and you had to work like a cart horse. Who helped you? Who brought you coal for heating? Your husband?"

Apparently Toni was surprised by the firmness of Rudi's voice, and her weeping stopped. She trembled. Rudi took her two trembling hands. He brought them to his lips and said, "You did the impossible. I will allow no one to torment you any longer."

Now Rudi saw, as in a thick fog, his father standing at the door in his full, mighty stature, throwing words into the narrow salon. Toni stood in the corner, her hands over her face, overcome with trembling. "On your responsibility!" The voice thundered and thundered. Apparently that was the only time Rudi met his father, clear and final.

Darkness fell on the roads, and Rudi made the horses race up the mountain. The path was clear, and the horses climbed with all their might. Rudi's determination to get his mother to the inn as soon as possible inspired the horses, too. They stumbled but surged forward, striving onward with their last bit of strength.

On the summit there was indeed a lighted wooden house. People stood at the windows. They seemed short in the tall windows, sunk in conversation.

"Fine," said Toni. "A fine house in a lovely spot."

"Let's go in," said Rudi, for he too was fatigued from the trip.

"Give me a moment to look at this splendor," Toni surprised him. "It's been a long time since I've seen such simple glory. It's hard for me to imagine this is a Jewish inn."

"Why?"

"Jews don't have a developed sense of beauty."

It was a wooden house wrapped in climbing vines. The shutters were painted dark brown, and there was a brass lantern at the entrance that immediately made one think of quiet rooms that give peace of mind.

"We have arrived," Toni announced in a tired, familiar tone.

No one came out to meet them. The people stood at the windows as though planted there on the alert. A middle-aged woman stood at a writing table and leafed through a book.

"Where is the landlady?" Toni asked at the entrance. All eyes were turned toward her at once, fixed on her.

"Pardon me. Have I made a mistake?"

"What do you want?" asked a man with a dry voice.

"A cup of coffee. We have come a long distance. We're thirsty."

Upon hearing that reply, without looking at her, the man turned his back.

"What did I do?" Toni asked in a choked voice.

"Pay him no mind," another man came up to her. It was evident he sought to rectify the bad impression. "I'll make you something to drink. What do you wish?"

"Coffee, please, if one is allowed to ask."

In the kitchen the people crowded around the stove and poured out boiling liquids. The evening light rested in the corners and softly illuminated the transparent jars on the upper shelves. They were glorious, self-possessed objects, bearing witness to quiet, pleasant days.

"Things are out of joint here," the man apologized. "But we'll still manage to get you a cup of coffee."

"What happened here?" Toni wondered.

"Haven't you heard? The landlady was killed, or rather murdered. Three days ago. Since then we have all been here, in shock."

"What did she do?" Toni asked unwisely.

"Nothing at all. A marvelous woman, everyone agrees.

She served the entire region without discrimination. You've never heard of Rosemarie?"

"They murdered her even though she had done no wrong?" Toni's voice shook.

"Just so, Madam, just so."

"Dreadful, simply dreadful." Toni could find no other words.

"Yes. Because she was a Jewess. The murderers did not disguise their wickedness. And since then we have all been distraught."

Strangely, their mourning was not at all visible. People stood in the lighted corners gobbling sandwiches and swigging coffee. The naked tables shone. They were old tables, delicately carved, well preserved, and even now, in their nudity, a noble smell arose from them.

"Where are the waiters?" Toni asked absentmindedly.

"No need. I will prepare it," the man said with his head bowed, going into the kitchen.

While Toni was still standing there in astonishment, a woman came up to her and said, "Where are you from, and where are you going, Madam? You are new, it seems."

"My name is Toni," Toni said in a low voice.

"My name is Tina. Pleased to meet you. Ever since Rosemarie was murdered, we have been lost. It is hard to describe the shock. Only poets, only great artists can do justice to these deep inner feelings." The woman spoke with natural fluency, somewhat rhetorically.

Toni bowed her head and said, "I'm very sorry."

"You should know, Madam, that Rosemarie was killed even though she had done no wrong. We can all attest to that. She was killed only because she was a Jewess. All the enlightened, if, indeed, they are enlightened, should declare themselves Jews. That is my opinion. Am I not right?

"Certainly," Toni said noncommittally.

"I never took special pride in my Jewish origins. I am not certain that the Jews are better than other nations. On the contrary, they have certain visible flaws that I condemn in no uncertain terms, but if someone is murdered because he is a Jew, then I proclaim myself Jewish in every respect. Am I not right?"

"Certainly you are right."

"I proposed to our friends that we write an open letter and publish it in the newspaper. We must not pass this over in silence. It is murder of the most blatant sort."

Her last sentence, spoken in a very intimate way, in the kind of words used to monger scandals and gossip, blunted the dread somewhat. Now the place seemed like a party in the home of a provincial artist who had decided to bring together old friends from afar.

"And who is this young man?" She addressed Toni in a whisper.

"He's my son."

"A comely lad, everyone agrees."

" 'Everyone agrees,' where have I heard that expression recently?" the thought flashed through Toni's mind.

"No doubt he's a medical student. What year, if I may ask?"

"He's still in school," Toni sought to ward off her evil eye.

"He looks like a man to me," said the woman, "a man among men."

"I've gotten you coffee and a sandwich, too," the man broke into their conversation. "The line was long, but if one has patience, one manages."

"Thank you, thank you with all my heart," Toni was embarrassed.

The woman fixed Toni with her two large eyes, said, "There is nothing more to say," and withdrew.

For a moment the air was charged with discomfort, but the man, seeing Toni's embarrassment, immediately began voicing his many concerns with increasing speed. "You must know, Madam, that I have been traveling this route for twenty years now, never without stopping here. I make it a rule to see Rosemarie's face at least once a year. A woman dwells in the very heart of the country and announces publicly: anyone whose heart thirsts may come to me, and I will nourish it, I will offer him a bed, a window, and a view, a new magazine, and a new painting by an artist whose star has just risen in the firmament of art."

"Marvelous," Toni said, feeling that the man was speaking with all his soul.

"With generosity, Madam, with love for anyone born in God's image, with openness of heart that sometimes bordered on extravagance. To give, that was her byword. And she kept to that byword faithfully. Why did I say 'byword'? Rosemarie never liked that word."

"No matter," Toni tried to make him feel better.

"Rosemarie was very sensitive to words. We, sinners that we are, use words as if they were clichés. Why aren't you drinking? The coffee is getting cold. It wasn't very hot in the first place. In three days everything has been destroyed. Unbelievable."

"And what are you going to do?" A hint of the man's enthusiasm had affected Toni.

"I have no idea. I, at any rate, have canceled all my appointments. I will not leave here until the matter is fully cleared up."

"You didn't give coffee to the young man? Doesn't he deserve a cup?" Tina burst in on them suddenly. "I will make some for him. Wait a moment. I'll make some for you. The long line doesn't frighten me. I've seen a few long lines in my life."

Chills went up Toni's spine upon hearing the woman's voice. She stretched both her hands out to the woman and said, "I can do without mine." But Tina would not give in. "They take care of everyone, but, for some reason, not of that lad. He is not thirsty. He is not hungry."

Her appeal made no impression. People stood on the stairs, in the doorways, near the kitchen. The house wasn't full, but it was humming with human activity.

"I said something, it seems to me. By now they have stopped responding to what people say to them. They are like beasts."

"I'll take care of him. I am his mother," Toni said foolishly. For it was just that word, spoken quietly, that drove Tina wild. She shouted, "You take care of him wonderfully!"

"What do you want?" Toni was startled.

"Simple concern for the young man."

Hearing that voice thundering through the rooms, Toni burst into tears.

"Pay no attention to that blabbermouth," a man said, placing himself between Toni and the other woman. "She can drive a person to distraction."

The woman was undeterred. "The lad before anyone else."

"Where are you, Rudi? Let's leave," Toni said as if he were not standing beside her.

"I'm here, mother. It's a fit of madness, pay no attention." Rudi spoke as one speaks to a crazed animal.

The man spoke in other terms, saying, "Because of one woman's madness, one does not leave shelter behind and set out into the night." That dry sentence made an impression on Toni. She gathered her hair together and her lips smiled. She said, "If you truly think so, I won't insist."

The people stood in corners and drank coffee from thin cups. Some of them held small glasses of alcohol in their hands. They were not drunk. On the contrary, there was a kind of closeness among them, as if before some family event, some nocturnal festivity.

"What shall we do, then?" Toni asked distractedly.

"You see? Nothing. What is there to do? Will words bring the dead to life? This place without Rosemarie turns us all into ghosts. She was a priestess," said the man, happy to have found the right word at last.

Rudi was enthralled. The antique lanterns, ornamented with Venetian glass shades, made him think of a long winter, the finest music, and the touch of thick wool carpets. He felt it: a hot current united the people wordlessly. They were under a spell.

There was a tall, transparent woman there with a poetic expression, who spoke lofty and incomprehensible words, aimed high. No one listened to her. The people stood riveted to their spots. Finally the woman put out her white hand as if she were about to perform a magic trick. It turned out she meant only to adduce proof, reliable proof of her Jewishness: her fingers.

No one laughed. Again, like a sorceress, with a kind of seriousness, she showed them her long fingers, apparently expecting a response. But that entreaty, or whatever one might call it, only froze the people more. No one uttered a word. "I take it back," she said, withdrawing to one of the unlit corners.

Rudi observed his mother's face again. Toni too was gripped by a kind of attentiveness. "We'll stay here. The darkness is thick. The horses are tired," she muttered as if to anesthetize a troublesome nerve.

After midnight Tina ceased grumbling, annoying, and

provoking. Her hands were full of work: she served coffee and sandwiches, as if her life had finally found a purpose. She offered Toni a tray with two sandwiches, saying, "Please pardon me. I intended no harm. I am utterly stupid. Please accept these sandwiches. Let me be sacrificed in place of the lad."

"Certainly I forgive you," Toni said with utter absent-mindedness.

"I feel better, I feel at ease." It seems she had not only brought food for Toni. She had also rushed to all the dark corners with trays bearing coffee. In the preceding days her feelings had apparently driven her out of her mind. Now she felt relieved.

The people sank into armchairs, closed their eyes, and dozed. "Drink, children, drink," Tina's urgent voice was heard. The hands desirous of drink had already fallen, white and tired, resting on the arms of the chairs. Occasionally a hand would reach out and ask, "Another cup." Tina roamed from room to room now, like a housewife to whom the night had brought beloved guests.

Meanwhile the man took the occasion to tell Toni all the events of his life during the past year. It had not been an easy one. Two years earlier he had been named chief representative of the famous Saenger Company. His joy had been great. He had celebrated the event, of course, at Rosemarie's. While his heart was happy with the festivities he promised Rosemarie that if he did well in business, he would give a scholarship to one of her beloved artists. At first he did do well, but malicious rumors had shaken people's faith. They stopped paying their debts. To avoid scandals or bringing suit against decent people, he paid out of his own pocket, hoping that the rumors would be proved false, that the storms would subside, and that understanding would once again reign as before. By the end of the winter it was already clear that his hopes were vain, worthless illusions. Then he had hoped Rosemarie would help him. She had connections in the area. That hope too was nipped in the bud. Now the firm would condemn him publicly as a thief.

"Don't worry," Toni said, as though she had fully grasped the complexities. "There's no reason to worry. Things will work out. It always seems we have no way out, and suddenly the way is opened. You will still award scholarships," she spoke forcibly.

"If I were a believer, it would be easier for me."

"No matter. Miracles also happen for the nonreligious. There are miracles for every one of us."

"Have they happened for you?" the man asked in wonder.

"Many, believe me."

The man lowered his head, and without asking any more he closed his eyes and fell asleep in the armchair.

"Wonder of wonders," Rudi said to himself. The small noises flowed into him with a kind of thrilling ease. Perhaps because he was awake, fully awake, as if his eyes were pried open. "There are miracles for every one of us." If he hadn't heard it with his own ears, he wouldn't have believed it. And the old remorse for not holding his mother at her true value, that hidden remorse, seemed to float up, rise, and throttle him. He wanted to stand up and ask forgiveness for the many years of intentional contempt. But he said nothing. "Mother," he said and leaned over, kissing her forehead. And Toni, who did not understand the meaning of that kiss, said, in fatigue: "Why not go to sleep? Upstairs there are certainly free beds."

No one slept in a bed that night. The rooms were laden with smoke, the fragrances of coffee and perfume. Toward morning the silence was broken by shrill laughter. The tall, blond woman who had presented her long fingers as a certain sign of her Jewishness the night before now sat in an armchair and giggled. A few people who were standing in the kitchen, enmeshed in sleep, grasped heavy mugs in their hands and put their heads out. Seeing the blond woman, they pulled their faces back like turtles in their shells. The blond woman muttered: "They murdered Rosemarie because she was a Jewess. What a laugh. She loved everybody without distinction. Did she discriminate between a Ruthenian, a Rumanian, or a Hungarian artist? True, she loved Jews too, and for that they murder a woman?" The thin light of morning now slipped carefully along the sleeping faces. It was a soft, summer light that, for some reason, reminded one of long vacations, boats, and young women.

Tina stopped asking people's forgiveness. She stood in the kitchen and poured liquids into thick mugs. The wild, crazy lines had been completely erased from her face. She now seemed like a worried mother, her stature reduced by apprehension. Her hands trembled slightly.

"Get up, children. There's coffee," she announced with concern. There was no need to rouse them. They were all awake, even those sprawled in the armchairs, but the blond woman, hearing the voice, opened her eyes wide and said, "And all this will remain empty, unpeopled." That announcement sounded ridiculous in the morning light.

Afterward the people stood around drinking coffee. "My name is Tortal," the chief representative introduced himself. His tired, unshaved face expressed a strange contentment. "Thank you very much, Madam, for the assistance you gave me. I was a lost soul."

"It was nothing, I did nothing," Toni blushed.

"You raised me up, Madam, from a deep chasm. Now I set forth with an open heart, without fear. Fear had compressed me like a vise."

Toni bowed her head. The words lavished upon her by the

chief representative pierced her. She wanted to flee him, but he did not withdraw. He stood by her, submissive and full of earnest thanks.

Finally she got away. She took a cup of hot coffee and some honeycake. The coffee's pungent smell reminded her of Prince Konicz, for they used to roast coffee beans in his house, grinding and sifting them before the fragrance faded.

"The coffee is excellent," she spoke to Tina as one speaks to a close friend.

"I am pleased," Tina said with utter simplicity.

For a long while people stood near the stove. The hot coffee eased their fatigue somewhat. Once again the disaster was forgotten, and they all busied themselves with complimenting Tina, who took great pleasure. But no one dared speak of the future. In vain Attorney Teicher tried to bring in the question of the future. No one wanted to hear it now.

At around nine Teicher put on his striped coat, placed his cap on his head, and stood at the door. His appearance was entirely unimpressive. His face now seemed dreadfully earnest, as did his summons: "Everyone out in the yard, outside for the memorial service."

The people slowly descended and crowded together near the stairs. Their faces, in the full light, seemed opaque. Twelve altogether. Standing in the courtyard of the house, surrounded by trees, they seemed even fewer.

"I came here every year. I never missed once," the chief representative confessed.

"I came twice a year, like clockwork, once in the spring, once in the winter," a tall man answered him. Until now he had not seemed tall. But in the yard, near the fresh grave, their voices suddenly fell silent. The blond woman, holding a candle in her hand, somehow seemed like a pious Christian.

She stood near a tree, shielding the yellow candle with both hands.

Some of the people wanted to break through the thin fence and prostrate themselves on the humid clods of earth. But no one dared. The wooden plaque and the fresh Gothic letters clearly showed that the grave was the end of all flesh. For a moment that simple truth enveloped the people and silenced them. Afterward, in the illuminated clearing again, the chief representative said once more: "It's a shame we're not religious people. The grave demands prayer." The blond woman laughed a thin laugh that sounded like a repressed cough. With her white hand she tried to cover her mouth. "How stupid of me," she reproached herself and turned aside.

There was no escaping the practical question of what would come next, who would guard the house, and, in particular, the spirit. Who would keep her spirit alive? Without Rosemarie everything was dust and ashes. The demands of reality came down and slapped the people in the face like damp rags. Once again it was Teicher who took the onerous task upon himself. "Pardon me," he apologized. "I am not a man of the spirit, but my heart tells me that we must not let this house die away in neglect." Strangely, it was he, who had not been considered one of the late woman's admirers, who took on the obligation. The others were frozen, or inundated with a feeling that it was all over. Toni too forgot herself for a moment, the trials of her journey and her oath. Those lost people suddenly became as close to her as brothers.

On the spot it was decided that a committee of three, headed by Attorney Teicher, would go to the village to hire a watchman for the house. The chief representative was actually willing to remain. But everyone prevailed upon him not to do so. It was preferable to have a guard at the gate. The three promised that upon their return to the city they would publish an advertisement in the newspaper publicly announcing that a high-minded person, a lover of books and paintings, someone affable who could attract people to poetry, was needed to manage the inn.

For a moment the sorrow was forgotten. As at any meeting, they drank coffee now, too. The meeting was held in the kitchen, adding a certain domesticity to the words and proposals that came from all sides. Some of the proposals were grandiose. Teicher wrote them down, but he did not consider them seriously. Like every practical man of integrity, he knew that imagination was of limited value, that an honest deal is not a glorious one.

To prevent their common will from being vain, Teicher asked that the Japanese plate be brought from the sideboard, proclaiming, "Let everyone donate as his heart dictates." Little time passed and the plate filled with bank notes. Toni took a bracelet from her wrist and placed it on the plate.

Teicher sat for a long time and made the reckoning. Of Toni's jewelry he said, "This is an expensive item. It will bring a good price." In the end he had the account circulated among all present. His insistence on formalities made Toni sad, as if it were not a question of simple protocol but of a spiritual accounting.

Now they were all about to disperse, some to the railway station, others to the village to rent wagons. There was a feeling of relief. Some seemed content, as if they had done their duty. The chief representative lit a cigarette and said, "That's that."

As the people were nearing the exit, Tina let out a shout, "Wait a moment! Where are you going?" Since no answer came, she hid her face in her hands and began to moan and weep. Her weeping was dry and frightening because of the logical arguments it stood for: "We are lending our hands to a crime. Three days ago a woman was murdered before our eyes, a woman who had done no wrong. The police refused to investigate, the head of the local council did not even bother to come, no one from the nearby village, whose people Rosemarie cared for when they were ill, not one of them came, and we are going away and locking the door. As if a murder that cries out to the very heavens had not been committed here! As if we were insects, not human beings!"

"What can we do? Wolves are better than the Ruthenians. Can you drive the wolves out of the forest?" Teicher tried to calm her down. The others also took the trouble of showering Tina with a welter of words. In the end she was reconciled. She closed the door, her practical tone returned, and she said, "Now you are going to the village, right? Allow me to join you."

The others started walking, as if after a nightmare, each in his own direction. In a short while only Toni and her son remained in the clearing. The carriage was ready, the horses alert. "It's lovely to be going off on a journey today," Toni said surprisingly. The shadows of the night were entirely wiped from her memory. Not so Rudi's. Now, with great clarity, he remembered the people who had surrounded him. A murky hatred for that tall, quiet man lurked within him. The man had not taken his eyes off Toni all night long. Though he had not approached her or said a word to her, Rudi sensed he had lusted for his mother grossly.

CHAPTER FOUR

The next day they left the plateau and the banks of the Prut and began climbing. Spring, vibrant with wind and water, was on those hilltops. The higher they reached, the louder the trees resounded with an earsplitting din. "Marvelous," Toni said, and tears welled up in her eyes. High mountains and tall trees always imbued her with a kind of religious awe. Yet in fact she was still immersed in thoughts of Rosemarie's abandoned inn. The night had reopened hidden wounds. In vain she tried to bandage them. From here everything seemed distant and frightening. She wanted to cling to her son and say a word to him. But she was afraid he would scold her for losing heart.

For a long while they journeyed without exchanging a word. Rudi too beheld visions of Rosemarie's bereaved inn before his eyes. The short men dressed in striped winter suits, the full-figured, overemotional women now seemed to him as though trapped in a snare they had built with their own hands. He remembered that at the beginning of the evening Tina had been a young, avid, shameless woman, but after midnight her face had changed color, and she became heavy, a woman who

had given birth to many children and was now concerned only
for them. Were it not for the tall, quiet man who had lusted
after Toni with his eyes, Rudi too would have taken part in
the conversation. That man's presence marred his feeling.

"Rudi?" she turned to him.

"What, Mother?"

"A penny for your thoughts."

"I'm thinking about last night. It was a long night, wasn't
it?"

The horses drove up and onward, and the night's visions
were gradually wiped from his mind. The horses, their breathing essence, once more filled him with joy. Not Toni. Sudden
fear fell upon her and pressed her into a corner. The steep
crests, the ravines and streambeds, all that dark greenery cut
into her flesh.

"What is it, Mother?"

"It frightens me," she said without shame.

Occasionally a peasant would emerge from the thickets
with a scythe on his shoulder, quiet and ready to spring like a
lurking beast. At that time Rudi did not know the ways of
that district, only what his mother had told him. She, in her
nostalgia, had painted her native land in rosy shades: a mild
climate, man and nature dwelling in harmony.

The fear made not only her hands tremble: she shook all
over. Furiously she chided herself. The chiding merely increased her irritation. Finally she asked him, "Stop the horses,
dear. I feel dizzy."

"What are you afraid of, Mother?" he bent over.

"I think about you all the time. I am no longer certain I
did right to bring you to this province. It isn't a peaceful region. Jews are persecuted here, and I have infected you with
that leprosy. Pardon this chatter of mine, but my fear is stronger
than I am."

"There's nothing to be afraid of. We've done no harm to anyone." He intentionally spoke briefly.

"True. You're right, but nevertheless Jews are persecuted. It has been their destiny from ancient days. You're fortunate, for you were born a Christian."

"Born a Christian." The phrase infuriated him. If that was the heritage left him by his father, better to deny it. He never thought of his father except to seek some expression of contempt.

"I am amazed at you!" He could not hold his tongue.

"Excuse your mother." She knew just what he was thinking. "I will conceal it no longer. In this region, Jews are not particularly well liked."

"So what?"

"Nothing." She withdrew into her coat. "Pardon me."

"We are Jews, and we will not hide that from anyone."

Toni lowered her head. The words struck her forcibly. His young pride was stronger than she, and, though she was certain he was not acting rightly, she said nothing. They got back onto the carriage and for a long time they traveled without exchanging a word.

The sky was brighter than before, cloudless. As they rounded a bend they met a Jewish peddler. He was startled when they suddenly stopped, and he stumbled. "Have you got coffee?" asked Rudi from high on his perch. Upon hearing German the peddler, not a young man, smiled and said, "I have."

"What quality?" Rudi called loudly, as if speaking with a deaf man.

"The choicest, from overseas."

"Would you show us?"

"Gladly," said the peddler, quickly undoing his parcel on the ground.

Rudi stepped down. Only when he stood close by did he

see how short the man was, no taller than a child. The odor
of his wares wafted from his thin body: soap, perfume, and
coffee. "Choice coffee, the kind you can't find any longer,"
he used familiar yet foreign words, Yiddish of course.

Afterward they went no farther. Rudi stopped near a stream
and loosed the horses. Toni spread a cloth on the ground.
Again they were enveloped in the babble of brooks. They had
black bread, cheese, and butter. Rudi gathered kindling and
lit a fire.

"I am so ashamed of my weakness," she said.

"What weakness are you talking about?"

"Coffee."

"Why do you call that a weakness?"

"I cannot do without it."

Before long Toni had a cup of fragrant coffee in her hand,
and a cigarette. Her faded face returned to life. It was as if all
the dread she had taken with her from Rosemarie's house was
now erased. Her skirt too suited her mood: spotted with red
polka dots.

Suddenly she raised her eyes and said, "You have grown
during the past year. Now you are five foot seven inches tall,
it seems to me—a fine height. Jews are usually short." That
was Toni's motherly voice, a moved, fearful one. "You have
gone your own way, and it is good that you have gone your
own way."

"What way are you talking about?"

"You are straight and sturdy. You are not moved except
for good reason. There is no hope for me."

Now Rudi felt the warmth of feelings in her being. He
could wish for no other mother, only one like her, in her
image. It was as if all the fault he used to find with her had
never been. She was his one and only mother, lovely and
beloved.

Toward evening they paused at a roadside inn. When Toni asked for coffee, the owner retorted that he ran a roadhouse, not a cafe. The innkeeper's brother was more brutish and made a comment about Toni's Jewishness. Rudi did not understand the words, but he felt their malevolence. "No one insults my mother," he said and punched him in the face. "Leave them alone," Toni was fearful and sought to restrain him, but Rudi was completely involved in his own anger, ready to stab and be stabbed. The boy's courage impressed them, as if an unpredicted force had caught them by surprise. They stood where they were and shouted curses that only showed how frightened they were. "Shut up!" Rudi shouted at them, and they fell silent.

As if for the first time, Toni realized he was no longer the child whose legs she used to wrap in a green woollen blanket, but a young man with instincts and a will.

They continued along the high plateau. The spring spread dark green along it. Mighty trees such as Toni had never seen in her life. It occurred to her that here nothing interfered with their growth, and that explained why they were so tall.

"Look how tall the trees are," she said, wishing to share her impression with him.

"So what," he said in dialect, the way a peasant might respond.

"I think they're delightful."

"What?" he said without absorbing her words. His entire being was given over to the gallop of the horses. They raced on now at an even pace. He was happy with them and with their full vigor.

"Rudi, do you hear?" She wished to attract his attention.

"What?" he opened his mouth.

"Why are you making the horses run so fast? It's hard for me to talk to you."

"Mother, they're running by themselves. I'm not doing anything to urge them on. They gallop beautifully, don't they? They're in top shape. It's good we bought them. I knew they wouldn't disappoint us." He spoke with pleasure, and that pleasure frightened her: he loves the horses more than me.

He changed from one day to the next. The sun and the wind shaped his face. His shoulders broadened. He gave off a strong odor of sour sweat, and he smelled of the horses. He would sit and chew his food for hours, as if he realized that patience and a blank mind were necessary for good digestion.

"Why don't you eat?" he would remember her from time to time. The food they bought from the farmers was too hard for her, even the cheese. It gave off a smell of earth and manure.

Sometimes a timid peddler would cross their path. His face and dress would give him away immediately. The peddlers informed them that the region was no longer as peaceful as before. The Ruthenians were in an uproar. Not far from there they had looted a Jewish inn, and the owner of the mill had fled for his life. "Don't go there," one of the peddlers warned them. Rudi smiled. The peddlers' frightened faces made him smile in a peculiar way, as if they were animals spoiled by having a roof over their heads.

Rudi and Toni did not heed the peddlers. They went on. Occasionally they would stop near a storehouse, buy some goods and water the horses. The Ruthenians noticed his gentile features and called him a German. They did not mistake Toni either: a Jewess who no longer kept the Jewish tradition. No one did them any harm. If a peasant dared call Toni a filthy Jew, Rudi would confront him fearlessly.

"I'm proud of you. Jews are usually cowards."

On their way they met lame and blind people, peasants

stripped of their land by nobles, drunks, and vagabonds, and, here and there, like a shadow, a fearful Jewish peddler. This is my land, Toni wanted to say, not quite the be all and end all, but not lacking a certain beauty.

On one of the mountains they met a French peasant from Alsace. In his youth he had joined the Mormons, and for several years he had relegated himself to alien and rootless climes. Finally he had cast anchor here and opened a hostel for wayfarers. He invited them in and served them a hot meal. After days of bumpy roads and dry bread, the country soup was like a delicacy.

From the Alsatian they learned that the region had been up in arms for months. Some Jews had been kidnapped by local ruffians. The man did not conceal his sympathy for the sufferers. His belief in the Jews was not abstract but rather a tenet of his faith. There could be no redemption of the world without the Jews. Those words had a strange tone in that remote and isolated place, where the winds and waters ruled unchecked.

Rudi was enchanted with the man and asked for information about his sect and its leaders, even trying to fit his tongue to French. The man spoke softly, courteously, as if he had absorbed the manners of the place and climate: no reason to rush. Toni did not understand a word. The stranger, who spoke a strange language slowly and in long phrases, suddenly made her fearful. "He must not speak," she wanted to shout. But instead she said, "What is the man saying? What does he want?"

"He is explaining that the Jews suffer though they have done no wrong."

"Interesting," Toni said, as if it were not a word of her own but one that somebody had lent her for a moment. They sank back into their conversation. The man revealed some of

his faith, and Rudi was pleased that he had managed to understand his interlocutor's French. For a moment he forgot his
mother, the bumpy journey, and the green vistas.

After their discussion of exalted topics they came back
down to daily necessities: horses and fodder, saddles and boots.
They ate thick sandwiches and drank beer, laughing long as
though they had been friends forever. Toni sat to the side and
watched them. She did not partake of the meal. Hot coffee
and a cigarette composed her thoughts. It seemed to her that
her son found great interest in everything connected to the
earth and animals. She was saddened. Her gloom turned into
suppressed rage. "He has forgotten me. And it is well that he
has forgotten me. I will leave him neither a high lineage nor
properties. Certainly not a good name. Better that he forget
his mother. The sooner the better for him."

"Mother," Rudi said, like a card player looking up from
his game for a moment. "Isn't it pleasant here?"

"Marvelous," Toni said, purposely exaggerating.

"The man has invited us to sleep here tonight."

"I would gladly stay here, but our time is precious."

"As you wish," he said, and turned back to his conversation.

Toni sat by the window. Only now, in truth, did she feel
that time had brought her back home. Not the Jewish inns or
the Jewish houses. Neither the smell of corn nor the autumn
had brought that pungent closeness back. Fear gripped her
narrow shoulders—not of what her parents might say, and not
what she might answer, but of the feeling of closeness, with
nowhere else to turn, like a brick thrown from a roof, waver-
ing for a moment but finally lying flat against the earth.

The feeling grew stronger, and slowly became a vision.
Her father and mother were sitting in the dining room. The
afternoon light splashed against the walls like sand. For hours

they had been sitting without saying a thing, as if they had
run out of words.

Suddenly her father raised his weary eyes, and her mother
understood that her husband was thirsty, and she hastily brought
him a cup of tea. Everything was in the same place, the table,
the chairs around it, the sideboard, and even the striped, rustic carpet. Only the silence was different. A silence made of a
heavy, translucent material. The eyes, with which they carried on short conversations. In fact, they were so attentive to
each other they had no need of that slight contact.

Toni was startled. She rose to her feet and said, "Rudi, we
must go." Rudi was clearly displeased by his mother's decision,
but he bent his will to hers, though not without twisting his
lips slightly. In vain the French peasant offered them a large
room with comfortable beds, cherries. Toni was gripped by
fear of that place. "We'll see each other again soon," she told
the man, for some reason, and they went on their way. "Pardon me for tearing you away from that conversation, but we
have no choice," she apologized.

"That man likes Jews."

"True," she said, careful not to contradict him.

Strangely, Rudi did not notice that she was secretly testing
him.

The horses had eaten well, and they skimmed along lightly.
Rudi showed no displeasure. He was given over to driving the
horses, and they devoured the distance with speed and assurance. The gallop completely overwhelmed his senses. "Thank
God he loves nature so much. He loves nature in a natural
way," she tried to console herself. In her heart she knew that
he was drawing further away from her day by day, not with
any malicious intent, but it was as if he were returning to the
estates bequeathed to him by his father.

"Pardon me for tearing you away from that conversation.

I would gladly have stayed. But time, you know, is not on our side."

"It doesn't matter," he said, unwittingly expressing his discontentment.

He snapped the whip over the horses' backs. The horses, apparently surprised by the whiplash, suddenly reared up. Now, in the evening light, she clearly discerned some of his father's features in him, his manner of sitting, his way of concentrating, or, rather, of ignoring her. She was anguished: it seemed to her that in a moment he would unsheathe his glance and stab her, like his father in the past. And he did indeed unsheathe his glance, but he looked at her softly, as if he knew just what she was thinking. "He forgives me," she said, feeling relieved. The thick spring darkness descended on the horizon. The few shadows were gradually swept away. In a short time all the stretches of light became darkness. Fear gripped Toni as in her childhood, and she wrapped herself in a wool blanket. "Aren't you afraid?" she asked unwisely.

"What is there to fear?"

"I'm glad I sent you to a good *Gymnasium*. There one learns well. There one learns sport. Sport strengthens the body. Fear is a despicable emotion. Jews are always fearful. It is good you are unafraid. I'm happy that you're not afraid."

"There's nothing to fear."

"Right you are. A sturdy son is his mother's pride." That was a slogan they used to embroider on thick linen cloth.

Rudi laughed out loud at the cliché.

"Am I wrong?"

"No. It's funny, it's just funny."

They journeyed all night long. It was not chilly, and no wind blew. Occasionally a dark breeze would brush their faces. When the dawn rose it was plain to see: they had taken a wrong turn. The darkness had led them into a dead end.

"I mixed you up," Toni placed the blame on herself. They were in a broad valley sunk in thick foliage. Mist spiraled up from the straw roofs. She wanted to say, "It's very beautiful." But instead she said, "Pardon me. I made you turn off the main road. I confused you. One must never talk while traveling, right?"

They ate breakfast in a poor peasant's hut. He could only offer them barley cakes and hot milk. Rudi was hungry and ate voraciously.

"Might you have coffee?" Toni asked and immediately regretted the question.

"No," said the peasant, baring his teeth in a grin.

Rudi narrowed his eyes as if to say, "You are truly hopeless."

Toni bent her head like someone justly rebuked.

"Where from and where to?" the peasant asked Toni.

"We are traveling to Dratscincz. Have you been there?"

"A pretty village, fertile lands. Are there Jews there?"

"There are. Not many. Are there any here?"

"There were, but they left. Many years ago."

Uttering the same "Dratscincz" sent shivers up her spine. For the first time after so many years she had pronounced the name of that place in the presence of a stranger. She wanted to ask when he had been there and whom he had visited, but seeing his broad, obtuse face, she did not dare. But the peasant dared. He asked, "Where's the lad from?"

"Austria."

"A fine lad." You could tell he was content not only with Rudi's stature but also with his way of eating. When Rudi finished his meal Toni handed the peasant a bank note. The peasant, seeing such a large sum come his way, doffed his hat in great embarrassment and cried out, "May God preserve you like the apple of His eye."

"Why did you ask the peasant for coffee?" Rudi asked when they were already well on their way.

"It was an error. I was confused. You know, desire for coffee drives me crazy. Ever since my childhood I have been addicted to coffee. Without coffee I go mad. You understand."

"Yes."

He did not mean to make fun of her, but that word, for some reason, hurt her feelings more than his question. Now, it seemed to her, he was mocking more than her weaknesses.

After an hour of galloping, he was himself again, and he saw he had behaved discourteously.

"Soon I'll make you a delicacy. You must be hungry." Toni was not hungry. Her longing for coffee secretly tortured her, but the torture was not unbearable. She smoked two cigarettes, and they dulled her desire.

Near the river they halted. Rudi lit a fire and made his mother a cup of coffee. "You drink too much coffee and smoke too much." For some reason he felt the need to preach to her.

"What can I do, darling? I am so nervous. Only coffee and cigarettes can calm me down slightly."

"Why are you nervous?"

"Don't you know, darling? All Jews are nervous."

He had noticed that in the past few weeks his mother had had nothing good to say about the Jews. On the contrary, she stressed only weaknesses and flaws. Once he had pointed that out to her, but she tenaciously kept to her opinion: Jews were no angels.

The weather smiled on them. Toni did not press him, and Rudi did not urge the horses on. At night they would light campfires near ruins or in open fields. At times it seemed they had forgotten the purpose of their journey. Rudi took care of the horses devotedly. He washed them and curried them. Toni would sit by herself for hours, staring, without thinking.

As they crossed the high, green plain she woke up: a ruined Jewish house. It was evening. The twilight sky still flick-
ered. Toni took her face in her hands and said, "This is a
Jewish house. That is what a Jewish house looks like."

"How do you know, Mother?"

"The windows, you see? They're wider."

"What else?"

"It's very similar to your grandmother and grandfather's
house. The yard. Even the trees."

The truth struck their eyes immediately. The doors, windows, and doorposts had been torn off, and only books were
inside, dozens of books scattered on the ground.

"I told you," Toni said. It was important to her to show
him she had been right at least once. "Jews always have a lot
of books. Only Jews have so many." It was a jumble of text-
books, novels, magazines bound up with cord, and children's
books. They were all in German except for a few religious
books in dark brown covers. The smell of mildew and the odor
of moldy paper filled the room.

"A geometry book," Rudi cried in amazement. "A geometry book in this desolate place!"

"Jews studied everything," Toni said.

"Why are you using the past tense?" he queried her.

"I?" Toni said. She did not catch his drift.

"I see a physics book too. What a joke."

"He doesn't intend to go on studying," the thought crossed
Toni's mind.

For a long time she stood rooted to the spot, so deeply
immersed in her thoughts that she didn't notice that Rudi had
gone out to light a fire. He knew: a cup of coffee would sweeten
her sadness.

"What are you doing, dear?" The words emerged from her
lips.

"A cup of coffee. You could do with a cup of coffee, it seems to me."

"So many books in one abandoned house. Where did the people disappear to?" Her voice trembled.

Rudi handed her the cup of coffee. There was softness in the way he served her. Toni took the cup and kissed his forehead.

"Two hundred and fifty miles to go. We could try a short cut, but I'm not sure the roads have been repaired. That's close, isn't it?"

Taking the short way, they could have arrived in two or three days.

The evening, the ruined house, brought her back to the moist soil. As if she had been born in that abandoned clearing. Great pity for her parents awoke within her. They had done their utmost so that their daughter could study. And she had wanted to study. She had made an effort, but it was in vain: her faculties betrayed her—and then afterward, the fear of failure, of being mocked.

"What will you study, darling?" she asked him in a voice not her own.

"I?" he was surprised. "I don't know. I'm not sure I want to."

"You have a brilliant mind. Everyone said so."

"Brilliant, you say?"

"Brilliant for studies, I mean. I, to my regret, brought great sorrow to my parents. Among other things, because I failed mathematics. You should know, dear, that among Jews studies are highly regarded."

"I love nature, and I'd like to live on a farm," he said in a tone she had never heard before.

"A farm, did you say?" she wanted his confirmation.

"I love animals."

"I always expected great things of you." An old anger fluttered within her. In fact it was not her anger, but that of her parents reincarnated within her. "Do as you please," she said in a weary, motherly voice, but within her she knew he was like his father in that as well. He had not yet discovered alcohol. When he discovered it, he would be enslaved to it like his father. "Do as your heart desires," she continued firmly, "but I have one request of you: stay away from beer and alcohol. They're poison. Drink wipes out the image of humanity."

"Mother, I never drink except at parties."

"Not a drop. Your mother suffered greatly from that. You know. I will not repeat myself."

"Why did you think of that just now?"

"Pardon me, pardon me. I'm anxious. Too anxious." Her anger dissipated, and she forgot about the matter. "Why don't you make me another cup of coffee?" She wanted to bring him close again.

"Gladly, Mother."

After making the coffee he watered and fed the horses. He lay on the ground like a farmer who has done his chores and fell asleep. "Why am I picking on him?" Toni spoke to herself in a housemaid's idiom. "Why am I tangling him up in all that? He has to live his own way."

The thick coffee dispelled her drowsiness. She sat and looked at Rudi as he slept. She listened to the noises and drove the evil thoughts from her mind. The long journey, jostling her from one place to another, now seemed like a tunnel with no exit. She longed for a warm room, a blanket, slippers, and a pillow she could hug. She had not forgotten her moments of splendor in Prince Konicz's apartment. But now he seemed ridiculous in his old striped suit.

The first light of day brought an itinerant Jewish salesman with its breezes. Toni was glad to see him, as if she had found a relative on foreign shores. The salesman too was pleased. He had been on the road for days. The road to the north was blocked. The Rumanian police no longer favored Jews. Bribes were ineffective. He spoke in short, emphatic sentences, impatiently. Toni served him a sandwich and fanned up the flames of the campfire. The salesman was hungry and took huge bites of the sandwich.

"Where are you going now?"

"Anywhere. Just not here. The Ruthenians and Rumanians are savages. I'll try to reach Austria, Holland. I have a cousin in Holland."

"And I have come from Austria."

"Just now?"

"Yes."

"God almighty. How can one leave a cultivated land and come to these mountains, these savages?"

"My parents live not far from here."

"Now I understand." He withdrew slightly as if hearing she was mortally ill.

Toni gave him coffee, saying, "I have no choice. I must return home. A person, ultimately, is not an insect."

"I understand," said the salesman with gravity, actually with fatigue.

Rudi had awakened from his sleep. He ignored the stranger's presence for a moment and went over to the horses. The horses, standing beside a tall acacia tree, immediately showed a kind of satisfaction at his fleeting touch. "Rudi, there's coffee. Let the horses be for a moment," Toni called. Rudi's gait was still ensnared in sleep, and in the morning light he looked slightly awkward.

"Mr. Kaplan, a traveling salesman, has told me all about the region. This is my son." The salesman opened his eyes again. Rudi's erect stature seemed to make an impression on him. Rudi grasped the cup and sat on the carriage seat like a cadet after maneuvers. Early manhood was fleshing out in him.

"The district is seething," the traveling salesman said. "Better let the fire die down. Savagery is rife everywhere. No law, no order."

"Coward," the thought crossed Rudi's mind.

"In civilized countries they are not fond of us either, but still it's better to be there than here. Here any drunken brute might swing an ax at you," he spoke dryly.

The man's thin aspect, the poor German he spoke, the way he sat, his miserable suitcase, and his broad hat upset Rudi's equanimity, and he asked in a quiet but rather sharp tone, "Are you afraid of drunks?"

"I? Of course I'm afraid. Do you trusts a drunk's discretion? A drunk is liable to swing an ax at you just because he feels like it."

"Drunks only curse. At most they swing bottles."

"True," the salesman quickly agreed with his statement. "Bottles are also dangerous. We, to our regret, are not built for that. A raised arm frightens us. What can you do? That's how we were educated. Maybe our parents are guilty too."

"Fear is not a noble feeling," Rudi spoke curtly in his annoyance.

"True," said the traveling salesman, and his miserable expression became even more so. "What can you do? Change the laws of nature?"

"The laws of nature aren't at issue, but rather confronting them."

"You are so right. You're absolutely correct," the man said, changing his tone and speaking to him as if to a peasant. And that put an end to the conversation. The wrinkles on the salesman's face shifted. A kind of mournfulness with a hint of irony covered his lips. For a long time he sat without uttering a word. Finally he got to his feet and said, "I'll be on my way."

"Why not drink another cup of coffee?" Toni pleaded with him.

"Thank you, Madam. I must hurry. To each his own. And time, you know, never stands still."

"As you wish," said Toni. She felt that the man was hurt, and she wanted to console him. "Take the sandwich. You will certainly be hungry on the way," she said in a motherly voice.

"Thank you," said the man. "I've had enough. I won't be any more bother to you."

The salesman quickly walked away. For a long while they sat without exchanging a word. "You shouldn't have spoken to him that way," she wanted to say, but she restrained herself. She made a few sandwiches. The contact with the black bread calmed her nerves. Rudi ate and drank wordlessly. The sun climbed, and its light filled the clearing, a wide and pleasant glade, surrounded by tall trees. A feeling of strangeness gripped her. "Why are you going away from me?" she wanted to protest but saw right away it would be silly. Rudi was the same as ever with her, just a small misunderstanding. She entered the ruined house. The scattered books lay mute, noiseless. For a moment her thoughts focused on this place and the people who had been uprooted from it. She imagined to herself that the owners of the house had been wealthy merchants, and in the winter each of them had sat in his own room reading magazines, while the girls prepared for school entrance examinations.

"Shall we go?" Rudi broke the silence.

"I'm ready," said Toni, and they went out.

The light accompanied them everywhere. Occasionally a peasant woman would appear out of a thicket and offer them early cherries or plums. Toni would speak to them in Ruthenian, and they would smile at the fluency of her speech.

"Whither?"

"Homeward."

Rudi kept his own counsel until the evening: "I dislike those salesmen. I find them repugnant."

"They're not bad," Toni said.

"Was I speaking of badness?"

"What can you do?" Toni found no other words.

"Sport. People who exercise don't sink to such a low level."

"Right you are," said Toni. Strange, Rudi did not notice that his mother was no longer using the words she had once used, but was choosing them more carefully.

The topic apparently perturbed him, for he said: "I don't understand what that fear is. A person could die of fear alone."

"He is referring to me," Toni thought. "I'm afraid of the slightest shadow, I have no courage. If I had courage, I wouldn't have sunk to this low level. Everyone cheated me, and I didn't write to mother." A chill ran up her spine. She wrapped herself in the blanket. Time passed, and the twilight, which had been prolonged for hours, was suddenly extinguished. Their faces were noiselessly plunged in darkness, and Rudi halted the horses.

CHAPTER FIVE

That night Toni knew she was quite close to her home. A peasant passed by and shouted: "Long live the king!" Two crows lurked nearby and snitched scraps of their meager repast. "We are close," she announced decisively.

Since they had left Rosemarie's inn, she had not been prey to changing moods. On the contrary, a certain desire to see, to observe her son's ways had taken hold of her. True, there were also fears. Some of her mother's nervous tics clung to her against her will. Everything, the light, the smell, told her she was steadily nearing the place she had left.

"In a short while it will be over," she said distractedly. She was pleased that the journey was drawing to a close. True, not as she had wished—though now she no longer clearly remembered what her original wish had been.

But Rudi was not content. The belligerent peasants clouded his spirit. He was storing up rage, and Toni feared its build-up.

"They are many, and we are few," Toni tried to make him understand.

"Does that mean they can do whatever they want?"

"Deep inside herself she knew he wouldn't understand. Perhaps it was good that he didn't understand. The suffering of the Jews was far from glorious. That night the word *goy* rose up from within her. She smiled as if hearing a distant memory. Her father would sometimes, though only occasionally, use that word to indicate hopeless obtuseness.

Rudi would tolerate no uncalled-for insults. The next morning, on the top of the mountain, a young peasant made as if to assault them. Rudi could have snapped his whip at him and driven on, but he chose to make a sharp turn, brake the spinning wheels, jump from the carriage, and confront the peasant face to face. The young peasant was thunderstruck and mumbled, "I didn't mean you, but the Jewess."

"What's he saying?" Rudi asked his mother.

"He apologized, he begged our pardon," she lied.

"Tell him he'd better not pick on anyone else."

Toni murmured a few meaningless words, and they went on their way.

"Strange, they sniff out the Jew in me. They have a highly developed sense of smell." She could not contain her amazement.

Once more they were on a mountainous plateau. Here and there was an empty Jewish house, a ruin, or a chapel. Occasionally a small flour mill would peep out of a ravine, powered by a waterfall, and the peasant standing by it would be taller and broader than his mill.

June was at its most splendid. From time to time a sudden cloudburst would fall on them, but the rain never lasted for hours on end. They would sleep outdoors or in an abandoned house. One night they slept in a synagogue. Seeing the deserted sanctuary, Toni took her head in her hands and said, "Lord almighty, why did the people leave Thy dwelling place?"

It was a narrow hall, open to the wind, and a few stained-glass windows still glowed high up near the ceiling. Rudi's expression was unmoved. Whiskers were spreading over his face, and, standing near the horses, his musculature made him seem like a coarse young peasant.

While the carriage sped on, a kind of dread descended upon Toni's shoulders. There was no apparent reason for it. She was not hungry, fearful, or angry—just a feeling of dread, plain and simple. She trembled. "Stop the horses, darling," she whispered.

"What's the matter, Mother?"

"I don't know. I feel dizzy."

Rudi halted the horses and gave her a pot of water. Toni washed her face. The journey, he noticed, had exhausted her. The blue veins near her temples, which he had loved to watch as a child, throbbed faster now. "I don't know what's the matter with me," she said.

"In a short while we'll get to a tavern," Rudi now spoke of the tavern as if it were their destination. He was tired of coffee. Now he yearned for a glass of draft beer, for men's talk.

They stood, bathed in the noon light. Toni hung a pendant around his neck, as though she were sure it was a safe haven for her precious jewel. In fact, she only wanted to give him something of hers, with her own hands. Rudi was hungry and thought only of a rich meal.

"Rudi," she said, "we are close to home. I want you to know that I have no fear. On the contrary. I am joyous. I'm certain that grandfather and grandmother have forgiven me."

Her emotion disturbed him, and he said, "Mother."

"I just wanted to tell you. True, I'm somewhat overcome with feeling. Everything here is so familiar to me, almost unchanged."

"But I won't go without a meal in the tavern."

"No, of course not. You must eat. You shall eat in the tavern they call The White Horse."

His hunger showed clearly. He lashed the horses' backs, and they devoured the road as if they had sprouted wings. Toni's eyes did not leave Rudi's hands. Now it seemed to her that those long, thin fingers would change beyond recognition. She felt sorry for all that beauty, which would disappear without a trace.

It was a handsome, two-story inn of brown and purple wood. The years had given the colors resilience, as if they had become drunk with the cold winds. On the lower floor a few peasants sat and drank beer. The barman did not ask what Rudi wanted. He guessed his wishes from his face and served him up a tankard of beer from the keg. Toni sat down next to him. A few drawings that she remembered from her childhood were still hanging on the walls. The years had improved them.

"Don't you want to drink, Mother?"

"No," Toni said. "I'll drink coffee afterward."

Rudi was completely absorbed by his hunger. Toni observed the way he broke his bread, dunked it in the gravy, and brought it to his mouth. "He's not nervous like me. Other, quiet blood flows in his veins. That is how a person should eat his meal, not as I do." She was less pleased with his drinking. She had to admit it to herself: overflowing with health. In the evening, without taking off his clothes, he lay down on the bed and fell asleep.

It was a dark and gloomy room, reeking of alcohol and tobacco, merely a waystation, not to be examined too closely. The mattresses were not the sort a sober person would enjoy laying his head upon. They were meant only for the tired and the drunk.

Toni was wide awake. Proximity to her home thrilled her.

She thought about neither her mother nor her father, but about the seamstress who used to come to their home in the winter and sew clothes. She was a thin woman whose slender fingers would race dextrously across the platform of the sewing machine. Toni had forgotten her name.

After midnight she opened the window. Not a sound was heard except for the murmur of the woods. The longer she stood, the fainter her sensations grew. She saw only the darkness gradually changing color.

When Rudi awoke from his slumber, light already covered everything, even the forest thickets. "I slept," he said, sitting up in his bed. A strong odor of sour sweat wafted from his disarrayed body.

"What'll we do today?" he asked, as if still asleep.

"Nothing. We'll rest a bit."

Without washing his face he went down to the horses. The horses expressed their satisfation with broken whinnying. Toni stood at the window and followed his movements. For a moment her entire attention was concentrated on what he was doing.

When he finished feeding the horses, he washed his hands at the pump, wiped his face with some water, and went into the tavern. The waiter, who did not understand German, brought Rudi an omelette with smoked sausage. Rudi ate it and ordered seconds. Toni was in no hurry to go downstairs. She knew her son was eating his heavy morning omelette now. After about an hour, since he still had not come upstairs, she went down.

Rudi noticed her and stood up. Toni seated herself next to him. The omelette, smothered in onions, disgusted her. "I'll wait outside, don't hurry," she said, and went outdoors.

The good light that had accompanied them all along their

way did not abandon them now. Toni figured she could reach her parents' house in two hours. For some reason that reckoning didn't hasten her. She stood in the empty clearing and looked at the old pine trees, rising up and casting their shadows on the earth.

After about an hour, since Rudi still hadn't come out, she went back in. To her surprise she found him standing and throwing darts at the round target. Rudi was also surprised. He put the darts down on the counter, and they went out.

"It's nice here," he said.

"I told you," motherly tones came back to her.

They had hardly gone out into the yard when that feeling of estrangement, which occasionally broke in and separated them, returned. She noticed that a different blue had settled in his azure eyes. But there was no blot other than that. He was handsome in the morning light, and his stance was solid and strong.

"You forgive me, don't you?"

"For what?"

"For this whole displacement."

He withdrew his glance from inside himself, and the softness she loved so much glistened in his look.

That was the last covenant sworn between them. Years afterward he would still recall the shadows of those high pines, his mother in her poplin frock seeking his forgiveness, and he, like an idiot, not understanding a word she said.

But for now he was deeply immersed in himself, as if in a slough. Now the two souls that constantly competed within him were completely split apart. The earthy soul was taking over. He ate and drank without pause, but mainly he drank. Toni's pleading had no effect. He did what he pleased; he was not in control of himself. Between meals he would throw darts or bowl with the peasants.

"You're drinking too much," she would try to reach him.

"Just a little more, and that's all." He would promise but not keep his promise. He was drawn to the beer as though hauled by ropes. He would not leave the bar until late at night. Toni would drag him upstairs to their room. Meanwhile she put off their departure from day to day. "As soon as Rudi feels better, we'll leave," she promised herself. Occasionally she would decide to scold him, to drag him away from the keg by force, but when she came to do it, her voice would quake, her hands fell slack, and she wrapped him in her arms as in the days when he was under her protection. He would not protest at her chidings. It was as if he sensed he had fallen asleep. His obedience pained her.

Days went by, and Toni did not manage to draw him out of the slough. His face was completely altered. An alien redness bloomed on the nape of his neck. "Don't you want to travel on?" she would try to rouse him. "Yes, certainly," he would mutter in his drunkenness. She tried everything to restore him to his former self. She was waiting for a miracle, and since it was long in coming, she stood next to the window for hours and prayed. "Oh, God, give me back my son, I have only one."

One night when she dragged him to the stairs with her last ounce of strength, he muttered angrily, "What do you want from me? Why do you bother me all the time?"

"Darling, I'm just bringing you upstairs so you'll sleep. Sleep will do you good." She noticed that his face had lost its softness. At times he scolded or ignored her. More and more he was sunk within himself. He even neglected the horses. Now she took care of them like a servant woman.

Between bouts of drunkenness and slumber he would wake up and be what he once was: a son one could sit next to and hug.

"What's the matter with you? Tell your mother what's bothering you."

"Nothing. I'm tired."

Many thoughts raced through her mind, but not one of them was of practical value. She became used to his drunkenness as one becomes used to a patient's illness, but she did not get used to his scolding. "Why did I bring him to this damned place?" she accused herself. As for her, it was as though her life had found a strange sort of penance, to wash his face and remove his shoes, and, if he had vomited, to clean up his vomit.

How would she reach home, or when? She did not think about that. Occasionally a drunken peasant would turn on her: "Dirty Jew." "Rudi, they're insulting me, I'm afraid," she sought his help, but he was so far removed in his drunkenness that it was doubtful whether he heard her plea.

Summer was over. Rudi would sit with his tankard and mutter broken phrases apparently remembered from school: "The Jews are the root of all evil." At night in the room she would beg him, "Don't talk that way. Your mother is Jewish."

"Don't say that. I hate the Jews. They are merchants and thieves." Now he spoke like a gentile.

That hostility continued for a few days. She learned to accept the insults and restrain herself. Though she didn't drink, something of his drunkenness infected her too. She stopped combing her hair and putting on make-up. More and more she stood by the window, without thinking, staring off into space. Occasionally she would go down to the stream and sit on the bank. In their room she talked to herself a lot: "A person is not an insect. I'm a hopeless coward. Rudi is right: the Jews don't know how to live honorably."

Autumn came, and with it the cold winds. The chill aroused Rudi from his drunkenness, and he asked, "Where are we?"

Toni was pleased at that question, as if the miracle had happened for her.

"Not far from home, dear."

"What home?" The dark cloud had left his brow, and spots of light sparkled on his face. Toni grasped his hands and kissed them.

The next morning he arose early and did not go down to the tavern. He sat on his bed. Toni asked him if he wanted to go for a walk, and he answered affirmatively. They walked along the river together. Rudi had grown taller. Were it not for certain delicate lines in his face, he would have looked like a young peasant. She wanted to ask him many things, but in the end she posed just a single question: "How do you feel?" After an hour's walk they took a short cut back to the inn. He slept for many hours. He slept on his ride side, all curled up. Toni did not leave his bedside. Toward evening he woke up, and Toni served him a cup of tea. She noticed that the blue of his eyes had grown somewhat clearer. He was weak and shut his eyes.

That night she knew that very soon she would return home. That clear knowledge no longer frightened her. On the contrary, now it became very important to her that Rudi know many details about his grandfather and grandmother, their sadness and their honesty.

When Rudi woke from his slumber, he stood erect, his eyes were clear, and his face expressed calm. For a long while he sat on the bed without uttering a word. Suddenly he got up, shook himself, and said in a clear voice: "Forgive me, Mother." "Why? I'm to blame. There's no need to beg my forgiveness. You did nothing wrong."

She immediately began telling him of the wonders she had thought about at night. But mainly she told him about his grandfather and grandmother. Toni noticed that the con-

cealed contempt with which he had measured her now left his
lips. A kind of surprise ringed his face. Toni's pleasure was
boundless. "Let's harness the horses and set out for the open
spaces. It's all over. It was just a nightmare." She wanted to
give free rein to her joy. But then and there she decided to go
alone. Better not take a chance. Better not panic her elderly
parents. She hadn't seen them in many years.

Before an hour had passed she found a wagon. The driver,
an old peasant, demanded no fare. He was traveling in that
direction anyway. Toni thanked him in their language and
lightly climbed up onto the wagon. Her raincoat was very be-
coming. He was later to think a great deal about that hasty
departure, about her large eyes, which, in the wide farm wagon, seemed fuller than usual.

Rudi went back to the inn. He bowled until late, playing
well. Between games he drank. Not too much. When it grew
dark he stood in the doorway and lit a cigarette. The cigarette
tasted pleasant in his mouth. While he drew in the smoke he
remembered their arrival there, the first night. He did not
recall the following days except as an expanse of thick fog.
Now the fog billowed within him, and he was thirsty.

Afterward he sat on a bench and listened to the night
noises. An autumnal calm pervaded the gardens and surrounded him as well. Of all the journey's many events, he
remembered only the kitchen of Rosemarie's inn now. That
glimmer of memory brought a smile to his lips, as if at the
memory of mischief long past. He did not think about his
mother. Even later, when he went up to his room and stood
at the window, breathing in the darkness of the night, he did
not think of his mother. He took off his clothes and fell asleep
easily. He slept late, and when he awoke the sun was high in
the sky, clear and round, without a blemish. The sky was a
thick blue, pleasant to look at.

He stood up and was pleased to be standing on his own two feet. Vapors of the strong drink burbled within him, but it was a quiet babble, not exhilarating. When he went out, the light flooded his face, and he felt vaguely remorseful. He stood up. Not a sound was heard around him, only the rustle of the morning.

He ate his breakfast quickly, swallowing thick pieces of black bread. The waiter asked Rudi something, but he didn't understand a word. He ate an omelette and again asked for a second helping. After the meal he went out to the horses. Contact with the thirsty animals roused his senses even further. He quickly splashed water on his face. The horses were pleased and expressed their contentment in joyful whinnies.

For a long time he stood by the horses as though fearing to leave them. A peasant came up and asked him a question. He was an old peasant and Rudi's foreignness aroused his curiosity. After a few efforts at conversation, the peasant smiled an embarrassed smile, excused himself, and withdrew into the shed.

Rudi opened the trunk of the carriage, took out two worn blankets, and spread them on the earth. A pungent, musty odor rose from the colorful blankets. He remembered how he had stood and folded them before their departure. Then the smell of naphthalene had wafted from them.

After cleaning the carriage and greasing the axles, he went into the inn. He ate a thick sandwich and drank a tankard of beer. "Where is my mother? Why is she taking so long to come?" he asked himself almost offhandedly. He stretched out his arms and looked at the spots of tar that clung to them. "No doubt she'll come soon," he tried to console himself, as if it were an afterthought. The light and warmth were at their fullest and enveloped his body. He returned to the horses, stretched out on one of the blankets, and fell asleep.

When he awoke the sun was already close to the horizon. He rose to his knees. He had slept deeply, and some time passed before he knew where he was. Meanwhile, a few wagons had gathered in the courtyard of the inn. Angry voices burst from the dining room, mingled with crows of triumph. The strangeness was very similar to that of a dream. In his dream he was very distant, among people whose language he didn't understand. He stood up and washed his face. The chilly water he drew from the hand pump roused him all at once. Now he knew that a day and a half had already passed since his mother had gone. That knowledge did not hasten his movements. He gathered up the blankets, folded them, and put them in the trunk. For a long time he sat bent over the maps. He found that the distance from the inn to Dratscincz was no more than fifteen miles. Within two hours he could be there. He had a desire to leave immediately, but he sensed it would be better to wait until morning. His reason overcame his desire, and he brought the horses back to the stable.

The next morning he rose very early, brought his suitcases down, and led the horses to the entrance. The leather boots encasing his feet altered his posture somewhat. He felt comfortable, and his self-assurance returned. He paid the cashier and gave the waiter a separate tip. The innkeeper, who wished to express his satisfaction with the guest, said in broken German, "Germans are good and also pleasant."

He covered several miles without meeting a soul. The road was narrow but paved, and he advanced confidently. As he rounded one of the bends he met a policeman. The policeman spoke a little German. Rudi asked him the way, and the man lavished explanatory gesticulations on him. Finally the policeman asked if he had a pack of cigarettes. Rudi got off the carriage, looked in the suitcase, and found a pack of the choice

cigarettes his mother had bought along the way. Overwhelmed with gratitude, the man removed his hat and thanked
him with head bent. That encounter, in the heart of the plain,
amused Rudi for a moment. A vulgar song they used to sing
at school came to his lips.

Afterward he rode straight ahead without asking direc-
tions and without delay. Images of the inn faded from his mind,
and as he advanced he felt that the wind and the horses were
emptying his mind even further. From time to time his mother
appeared before him, dressed in her raincoat, as if, over all
the years, that had been her only costume. He was surprised
at her untimely appearance, but in the end he found her beautiful; her brow was pure, unstained. The road was longer than
he had reckoned. Though he did not urge the horses on, they
galloped, a gallop of joy as if after a long imprisonment.
Nevertheless he managed to absorb the autumn quiet loveli-
ness, to breathe in the widespread decay of the fruit, and to
say to himself, "Everything is beautiful here."

Reaching the top of an incline, he remembered that when
he was fourteen he had had to choose between a military academy or the *Gymnasium*. He had leaned toward the military
academy, and his mother toward the *Gymnasium*. His mother
had felt that the military academy would be too strict, the
school was far away, the vacations were short, and then he
would be sent off to guard the frontiers. All the disadvantages
his mother had found in the military academy seemed like
advantages to him. He loved sports and faraway places. In the
end he bowed to his mother's wishes and registered in the
Gymnasium. After a while their differences of opinion were
forgotten. He did well in school, and if it had not been for his
mother's wanderlust, he would have graduated. Now he was
sorry he had not had his own way.

"To go and not return on time," he thought, a kind of suppressed anger twitching within him. "You can be an hour or two late, but not a whole day." Now it was not entirely anger. The landscape spread the full range of autumn colors before him: a flush of red, yellow, and rust. That splendor softened the eruption within him. In fact he was content, for he had returned to his beloved horses, and that contentment filled his being with an old happiness. As he advanced it was as though he had forgotten the purpose of the journey. The slumbering powers of youth were aroused in his limbs. If he had met a girl, he would have stopped the horses. From time to time a wagon laden with hay passed by him, a peasant dozing in his seat, as if there were no dangers in the world.

He reached the village toward evening. He knew he had arrived. The thatched huts scattered about, the thin smoke, and the swirls of dust raised by the beasts on their way back from the pasture captured his eye, and he forgot himself for a moment. He immediately realized that this was the place. It was hard for him to pronounce the name, but he pronounced it. A little girl standing by the side of the road affirmed it wordlessly: yes, Dratscincz.

He had heard about that light since he was weaned. His mother had preached to him about the secret existence of this distant place, like a lost object that had to be restored. She was capricious, and he hadn't believed her. But the legend was stronger than he, and it lodged within him against his will.

Now he saw it: a village with a few trees at its feet, the wind tossing their branches, smoke curling up from chimneys, animals scattered about, and an open square, apparently the marketplace.

If you return home
You will find that nothing has changed,
Everything is in its old place,
Even the fences.

That was the chorus, or rather the anthem, that his mother had sometimes sung to him at his bedside in the evening. A Ruthenian melody to which his mother had adapted German words. He stopped the wagon, and the words burst out from within him. He was certain his mother would hear his voice and joyfully come outside. But nothing moved. A few peasants sat beside their houses, resting on long mats. From time to time a horse's neighing or a child's weeping would break out. The smell of bread hung in the air.

For a long while he drove through the village without slowing down. Although he could not identify any of the precious sights his mother had told him about, he seemed to be familiar with every corner. If he had known Ruthenian he would have stepped down, watered the horses, and bought a loaf of bread. He yearned for bread baked in the round village ovens. But no one was outdoors. The evening light had a pleasant feel, and as night fell, it grew bluer.

A woman passed by, and he called from his seat: "Rosenfeld." He was sure the woman would reply immediately, put out her hand, and show him the direction, but she stood as if an obscure and impenetrable word had been whispered in her ear. "Rosenfeld," he called out again, distinctly and softly. Now it was clear to him that his voice was falling on deaf ears. "Pardon me," he tipped his cap. The heavy woman smiled, revealing her teeth, as if a foolish acquaintance had crossed her path. He proceeded slowly, as if the day were not drained away and evening about to fall. He was enchanted by the sunset and forgot not only time but also his mother. If he had

seen a young woman nearby he would have stopped the wagon
and gone into her house. Faint yearnings always aroused desire
for a woman in him. But none came his way. Big, heavy women
stood in the doorways next to animals bound in chains. A
kind of wonder floated up from their eyes, as if some of the
bound animals' resignation clung to them.

"Where are the Jews?" he wondered distractedly. "Where
are they? Can the place be empty of Jews at this hour?" In the
whole expanse there was no light indicating a shop or store.
The village houses, crowned with thatched roofs, grew pro-
gressively grayer, and as he drew near them they seemed more
like stables than human dwellings.

Darkness fell suddenly. Tiny, faint lights poked out of the
low houses. The sounds grew fainter, and the smell of water
mixed with that of mowed grass spread through the air.

Still seeking his way, he saw a stone building with a lantern at its door. He stopped the carriage and examined the
door from his seat: was it an inn or a tavern? He pulled the
carriage to the side and went in.

"Does anyone here speak German?" he asked loudly.

"A little," answered a policeman in a low voice as he stood up.

"Where am I, if I may ask?"

"Your worship is in the police station. How can I be of
assistance?"

"Thank you." Rudi resumed his old voice. "What is the
name of this place?"

"Dratscincz, not a famous village or one known for its glory."

"Then I've come to the right place."

"I am pleased," said the elderly man. "Take a seat, and
permit me to serve you a cup of coffee."

The old man spoke broken but understandable German.
He quickly brought a cup of coffee and served it with trembling hands. "How can I be of assistance? In my youth I spent

half a year in Austria. I took the police training course." He spoke with a homely singsong, as they doubtless spoke in the village.

"You speak a fine German," said Rudi, who liked the lilting accent.

"Thank you." The man was pleased with the compliment. "Whom are you seeking in this darkness?"

"The Rosenfeld family. Would you be so kind as to direct me?"

"Willingly. It's not far from here. Near the flour mill. But drink your coffee first, rest a bit, you've been traveling."

"How many years have you served here?"

"Many years. Once this region belonged to Austria, and we hope it will soon return to her. German is the language of culture. We, to our regret, have no real language." He sought to ingratiate himself somewhat. They sat for a long while. Rudi was tired and that monotonous murmur dripped upon his ears without arousing his emotions. With a wealth of detail, the man recounted everything he had done in his youth—a gay youth, apparently. In his fatigue Rudi wanted to ask him whether there was an inn nearby, but then he remembered that he had come to meet his mother there, it was late, and in the village people went to sleep early.

"Would you be so kind as to show me the way?" he got up and asked hastily.

"Certainly," the policeman said softly. "I'll go with you so you don't get lost."

"My mother decided to come ahead of me. I assumed she is worried. No matter, we'll surprise her," he said with a kind of light, youthful pride. "Is it far from here?"

"No, nearby, but no one is there."

"What do you mean? Have they gone for a walk?" he bantered.

"They were deported, sir. Today they were deported. You didn't know?"

"I don't understand." Rudi said.

"You don't know?" He was surprised. Putting his official cap on his head he said, "You don't know that the Jews were sent away by order of the governor?"

"Where?"

"I don't know. We had a very limited task. To gather them up."

"Why?"

"Because they are Jews, sir. Do I have to explain to you?"

"Let's go and see," Rudi said, using the first-person plural, as though he sought additional eyes to bear witness to the impossible. But the policeman was right. It was a good-sized house, and the windows gaped into the darkness. Rudi lit the empty, peeling interior with the lantern. Books and coats were scattered all over the floor.

"You didn't know at all?" the policeman was surprised.

"No. Now I'll have to look for them. Where can I look in this darkness?"

"It's very simple." The policeman tried to mollify him. "Go straight, without turning, to the railroad station."

"What harm did they do? Why were they driven out?" he was outraged.

"They are Jews," said the policeman.

"My mother is a very honest woman. She never harmed a soul."

"They will certainly free her immediately. It is only a matter of the locals. They will free the foreigners immediately." The policeman was now piling up his words hastily.

"Now I have a trip in front of me," Rudi said to himself.

"You may sleep here, if you wish. It is not an elegant place, but there is a bed."

"I'll travel on," he decided at once.

"I understand," said the policeman. He felt Rudi's repressed rage. "Have a safe trip, if that is your wish. May God preserve you."

Once more he was in the open fields, hungry and devoid of any emotion. A faint feeling told him his mother had fooled him. How and why, of course, he did not know. He was sorry he had not asked for more details about the expulsion. Now, in the darkness, he saw what he had not seen in daylight, the faint cunning that had hovered about the old policeman's lips. The fact is, he had not known what to ask. For some reason he had been embarrassed. The policeman, with great astuteness, had not offered many details, he recalled. The night was quiet, without wind or rain. Toward morning rain fell, and he wrapped himself in a piece of canvas. The impermeable canvas warmed him, and he fell asleep. In the morning he reached the railroad station. He was late. The deportees had already been sent on. In the tavern they told him that during the day the Jews from the entire surrounding area had been gathered, and toward evening they had been moved to the railroad station. Several peasants, two policemen, and a woman who spoke a servant's German joined in the explanation.

Rudi was hungry. All his wishes were focused on that one desire. "How far is the next railroad station?" he asked. The barman's answer was like that of a peasant, "A two-hour ride in a carriage like yours." He ate an omelette with smoked meat. He had a huge appetite and ordered a second portion. After finishing the meal he smoked a cigarette and dozed off in his seat. He slept no more than an hour. When he awoke panic struck him: "Where am I?"

He immediately found out the direction and set forth. He covered the distance in an hour. It was an old-fashioned railway station, neglected, holding a mixture of people, iron beams, and casks. Now the Jews were there, too. In the crowd of people it was impossible to see a thing. They were all draped in fatigue and apathy.

"Where is the office, where is the man in charge?" he burst in. No one threatened to do him any harm. On the contrary, there was a willingness to assist him. "Mother!" he shouted into the mass. "Mother." For a moment that loud cry frightened the deportees, who were sitting on their bundles.

"Can you help me?" he addressed the officer.

"In what way?" the man spoke to him courteously.

"I have lost my mother."

"Don't worry. She isn't here. These are Jews."

Strangely, the answer dispelled his worry all at once. He looked at those miserable faces distantly. As though it had become clear to him beyond any doubt that his beloved mother could not be among those wretches. They would go off to their fate, and he would seek his mother elsewhere. A kind of relief enveloped him.

"Could you give me a little water?" a woman addressed him in a soft, very domestic voice.

"I have none, don't you see I have none?" he shook off the plea.

"Pardon me," said the woman, bowing her head.

While he was standing in amazement, a little freight train appeared. The people got to their feet and stood, as if they realized the train was meant for them. Some of the taller men, bearing loaded packs, put out long arms to indicate their willingness to do what they were told. The policemen surrounded the cluster on all sides. They apparently intended to push them, but there was no need. The railway cars easily sucked them in. Hardly a few minutes passed, and not a soul was left in the open area.

The policemen left the platform and went into the cafeteria. The owner of the cafeteria announced: "The sand-wiches are ready, the beer keg has just been tapped." The policemen did not appear enthusiastic. They stood at the door of the cafeteria and lit cigarettes. It was as if they had long been awaiting that moment when they could suck in the smoke with pleasure.

Rudi did not delay. He set out. He didn't know where. For a long time he drove without seeing or feeling anything. Only after nightfall did the sights appear before his eyes again: men, women, and children, wrapped up with their parcels. Ex-hausted wretchedness that sometimes seemed like a prolonged blank stare.

He spent the night in a field with the horses. It was cold, but the cold did not deprive him of sleep. When he awoke the light was still wrapped in the vapors of night. He lit a fire and drank coffee. The hot beverage summoned his mother's face, as if by magic. "Why didn't she wait for me?" the angry thought passed through his mind. "And how can I find her in this wild land?" He got to his feet, put the pot in the trunk, and set out. The whole matter, which had seemed like a mis-understanding the day before, gaped before him like a deep chasm. The cold had penetrated his bones at night, and now he felt it.

In the afternoon he stopped at a small railway station. "Where are the Jews?" he asked the cafeteria owner.

"Who knows? They took them away."

"Where? I ask you."

"You're asking me?" The cafeteria owner was surprised.

Rudi wanted to slap his face, but the rage that was clenched in his fists weakened him. He stood on the empty platform. The will to act that he had felt at night, in his sleep, dissolved within him. He stood near the horses, empty of desire. For a long time he stood, enveloped in the cold light. His hunger

died away, and he looked at the idle policemen standing near
the buffet. Their expression was not one of malice or evil.
They stood like peasants at the door of their houses. After
about an hour he got up and went out to the tracks. He drove
without urging the horses on, with painless devotion. Near a
tavern he stopped. He had two drinks. The liquor made him
slightly dizzy, but he was alert, fully alert, and the longer he
sat, the clearer his awareness grew. He suddenly understood
what he had only guessed in secret: his mother was in danger.

CHAPTER SIX

He wandered from place to place, not knowing whether he was heading north or south. The stations all resembled one another, the same inspectors, and the same policemen. The same whores unabashedly offered their flesh. He learned a few words of Ruthenian the way you learn the prisoners' language in jail. He did not find his mother. Her face fled before him, and only at night did it draw close to him, like a thirsty bird drawn to a body of water.

Occasionally he got drunk, hit and was hit, but his mind remained steadfast. He cared for the horses as though he owed them a debt. He did not stop criticizing his mother, even as he longed for her. She was always late, her plans always went awry. Over the days his criticism grew more temperate, but it did not cease. A change took place in him, too, in his posture, in the way he ate and fed the horses, in the way he remembered. For hours he would sit beneath the carriage and look around him. A certain feverish sentiment already burned within him, but he took it for a passing feeling. The peasants regarded him as one of their own, and they never suspected him of being foreign. At barriers they would let him pass without checking his documents. The war was already in full tilt, but there was no trace of it here. Except for the railway stations daily absorbing the deportees, the peaceful autumn reigned with its welter of colors.

From time to time a woman resembling his mother would slip by him. They were Jewish woman running away from the railway stations, thin and frightened, crossing the paths, clinging to the fences and dissolving into the dark greenery.

"What do they want of them?" he asked one of the policemen in easy German, so he would understand.

"They're Jews," said the policeman without batting an eye.

"Where are they taking them?"

"To their fate."

"What does that mean?"

"I don't know. Certainly it is God's will."

"You mustn't torture people," Rudi could not restrain himself. "You're right," said the policeman. "But it's not in our hands."

One evening he saw a young girl next to a tree. She was so frightened she didn't even try to escape. She clutched the tree trunk as though she were drowning. "My name is Rudi," he called. His shout apparently alarmed her even more, and she sank to the ground. "Don't kill me."

"What are you talking about?" he said, sinking to his own knees.

"I'm frightened," she managed to say as she fell.

He drew near her on his bent legs. She did not move. "Let her rest a little," he said to himself and went back to the horses to water them. The horses were thirsty and gulped the water from the bucket avidly.

After about an hour, since she had not stirred, he took out his mother's winter coat, a striped wool coat, and covered her. Everything that had happened to him recently seemed like a dream, and his search for his mother also seemed like a blind man's gropings. Now it seemed that the girl was bringing him a kind of hidden promise. He lit the fire and boiled water in the pot. That act, which he did out of habit, completely unthinkingly, evoked his mother's face in strong light. He saw her up close: her face as it always was, a broad brimmed hat on her head, thin happiness on her lips.

Night fell and he wrapped himself in a blanket. The strong coffee woke him up completely. He saw the way he had traveled with his mother before his eyes: Rosemarie's hostel emptying out, the horrible inn. Fear that his mother would be lost to him in that green desert brought him to his feet. He approached the horses. Night spread out, dark and humid.

When the sun shone again the girl suddenly rose to her feet and stood. Rudi was astonished but restrained himself and said in a soft voice: "Good morning." Hearing Rudi's voice, she turned her head. It looked tiny on her narrow shoulders.

"I have a cup of hot coffee," he said.

"Pardon me," she said, and she smiled immediately, as if realizing that was not how one should respond.

Rudi prepared a cup of coffee for her. She took the cup without a word and brought it to her lips.

"Hot," she said. "Good."

"Where are you from?"

"From the railway station. We waited for a long time, and no one came to take us. I was thirsty and went to get a drink of water."

She seemed to be about thirteen, but by the tall tree she seemed even younger. Wonder covered her face.

"You ran away."

"No. My mother told me to go to the well and fetch water, and when I came back no one was there."

"Since then you've been wandering."

"Yes. How did you know?" Her eyes were even more surprised. Fear left her, and she sat down. Her thin, tan face took on a blunt opacity.

"What's your name?"

"My name is Arna. Everyone calls me Arna."

The morning light was now dark and wet, and low clouds wandered over the treetops. Rudi gave her his mother's green wool jacket. She wrapped herself in it. The jacket covered her legs.

"I shouldn't be scattering my mother's clothing," an angry reflection crossed his mind.

"And you, where are you from?" she addressed him unexpectedly.

"From far away."

"Are you Jewish?"

'Yes."

A smile spread on her face. "You don't look like a Jew."

"Why?"

"I don't know."

Rudi drew water from the well, cleaned the horses and gave them fodder. The hope that the girl brought him good tidings faded from his heart. Once more he was on his own, with his hunger, with the preparation of a cabbage salad. When he finished the chore he said, without looking at her, "Eat something."

"Yes. I'm hungry."

He gave her bread, cabbage salad, and smoked meat.

"Dumb kid," the thought crossed Rudi's mind. She ate it all. A coarse smile of satisfaction wrinkled her lips for a moment.

"And what do you plan to do?" he asked.

"I don't know. My parents will certainly find me. They haven't abandoned me. They love me."

"Do you have brothers and sisters?"

"Yes, two little brothers. They cried all the time and drove Mommy out of her mind. There were a lot of people at the station. Daddy spanked them, but they only cried louder."

"Do you love them?"

"Yes. But I love my mother more."

He could have told her, "Go your own way. Your parents will certainly find you." Or else just harness the horses and leave her behind. She wouldn't have asked for mercy. He didn't do it. Not that his heart didn't tempt him to, but you don't drive away a stray dog that has attached itself to you.

"Get on," he said, and she got on.

He headed north and immediately changed course. He stopped at a nearby railway station and asked whether they had deported Jews from there. The cafeteria owner's answer was clear: "A few days ago. Not many. On a freight train." He inquired, though his heart refused to believe that his beautiful mother's fate would be like that of those wretched souls he had seen with his own eyes.

When he came back from the station he asked Arna, "How do you feel?"

"Fine," she said. "I feel asleep."

"I brought you some cake."

"Nice cake," she said and took it from his hand.

He went on. The autumn gave clear signs of its presence: fog and drizzle. With difficulty he mounted the canvas over the carriage, and the effort left him slack and listless. Longing for his mother filled him with strong pain. "Mother, where are you? Give me a sign, and I'll drive that way. Without any sign, I can't reach you." No sign was given. More than anything he set out so as not to stay in one place.

"What do the Jews do on Saturday?"

"Don't you know? They light candles. Mommy is very observant. Bud Daddy never goes to synagogue. Not even on Rosh Hashanah."

"And do you believe in God?"

"Yes, why are you asking?" She was frightened.

The motion of the carriage would put her to sleep. Sometimes he would stop the carriage and look at her: a narrow face, a flat nose bent slightly to the right, long ears, dark brown hair. Not terribly pretty. But she was quiet and didn't get in the way. As if she understood that two little brothers annoying her mother with their screaming were enough of a burden. She, at any rate, would not be a burden to anyone.

He drove and his mind wandered. Occasionally he would need a bottle, but not to get drunk. His mind was so clear he could remember the whispered muttering of his mother. "They are different, certainly they are different," he would hear his mother's voice. "They have a certain hidden advantage, isn't that so?" But he did not forget that his mother was also more than a little critical of the Jews' way of life. All that had come and gone. Now, from Arna, he learned other secrets. "On the eighth day of their life they circumcise them, didn't you know?" she told him.

Imperceptibly the rain became hail. They slept in the empty, plundered houses of the Jews. There was no lack of books in them. In one of them he found a full, well-bound set of Gratz's *History of the Jews*. He took it with him.

Arna quickly learned how to do all the chores and was no bother. She learned to feed and water the horses, to make coffee in the morning, and even to bake bread. Every week he would sell one of his mother's garments and buy supplies. He didn't touch the bag of jewels. He tied it around his neck and swore to himself: "Until I find her I will not remove it from my neck."

Occasionally they would encounter a Jewish woman or child, slipping past them like forest shadows. The thought that those shadows, fleeting past him in dread, knew the secret gave him no rest. Around one bend a woman scurried past him, and he decided to chase her. He ran after the woman for a long time, but she was quicker than he and evaded him. He came back angry. Arna learned to squeeze her body into the trunk in the rear. She didn't speak unless spoken to and then only a few words. At one point he asked her whether the peasants had beaten her. In response she bared her right leg, showing him a broad wound, dripping with pus.

"Why didn't you tell me?"

"No matter. Now it hurts less."

The frost grew sharper daily. The campfires did not warm them. Arna was the only living soul with whom he exchanged a word. But it was hard for her to talk. Rather, she did not know how to respond. Why were they deporting the Jews? Where were they sending them? That was a tangle with no way out. And in that fog his thoughts were increasingly stifled, though about his mother there was great clarity. He remembered the hasty packing, the speeding train, and how her feet touched the soil of her homeland. There was something religious in that return. And later in the Jewish inns, bright havens where she had met people and been very moved. Then he felt ill. He sped along the plains thinking that the cold air would heal him, but the illness was stronger than he, and in the end he felt weak-kneed and chilled. He could no longer stand on his feet. Arna was alarmed, but like a girl from a poor home burdened with children, she quickly recovered, lit a fire, and made him a cup of boiling tea.

Night fell upon them near an abandoned Jewish home. It was a wide house with the windows and doors knocked out, a few religious books on the floor. Arna lay Rudi in a corner and covered him with two blankets. She blocked up the windows with sacks.

"What can I give you?" she asked again and again. He muttered bits of speech whose meaning she could not grasp. Finally she placed a damp cloth on his forehead, and he stopped muttering.

Morning came and Rudi did not open his eyes. Arna sat without taking her eyes off him. She was waiting for him to utter a sound, and since he said nothing, she trickled tea into his mouth drop by drop. "He's very pale. He's very sick," worry whispered in her mind. Even in her alarm Arna didn't forget about the horses. She quietly took care of them, and the horses expressed their contentment. A kind of practicality she had inherited from her mother guided her fingers. She did not budge from him even at night, when the darkness was complete. Many thoughts wandered through Arna's mind. She thought about her mother and father, her two little brothers, but more than anything she worried about her mother. She saw her father as he always was: with an angry face.

"Mother, Mother," Rudi murmured feverishly. "He's very weak," Arna said to herself and mashed an apple. She was sure that an apple would cure him, perhaps because once when she was very ill her mother had bent over her and whispered: "Taste this." It had been applesauce.

But the frost outside could not be resisted. From day to day the north wind grew stronger, finally bringing a snow-storm. Arna did not sit idly by. She sealed the windows and doors with sacks and rags, and she brought the horses inside. Better a broken house than no house at all.

"I want to die," she heard Rudi's voice.

"You can't," she scolded him loudly so her voice would penetrate to him. Within herself she decided: "I will not allow him to die." She had inherited that resoluteness from her mother. Her mother had not left her children's bedside when they were ill. She filled a bottle with boiling water and put it at his feet. For hours she sat next to him, unreflecting. Thought had ceased to flow. She riveted her eyes to his face. "He will get better, he will recover," her lips murmured. One evening the prayer, "Hear, O Israel," broke from her lips.

For a week Rudi wrestled with the angel of death. Arna cared for him the best her hands knew how. She wrapped his chest in warm sweaters and coats, but the cold wind broke through, for she could not block it. It reached through every crack.

After a week Rudi opened his eyes and asked: "Where am I?"

"Here."

He shut his eyes again.

She felt relieved. Utterly exhausted, she wept and fell asleep. When she woke up it was already completely dark. The horses breathed in a whisper. In her sleep she had been bundled up next to her mother. She remembered that her mother had given her much advice, but it had been erased from her memory. Rudi too had been in her dream, healthy and sound, sitting next to a campfire and roasting potatoes, his face bright and unspotted.

When day broke her eyes saw that the ruined house was completely buried in the snow. The doors and windows were sealed up, and only the back door, which was sheltered, offered an exit. For a moment she wanted to consult with Rudi, but she immediately realized her error: he must sleep. "It's a good thing I'm here," she said without knowing what she was talking about. The food was running out. She ate very little, only once a day, two roasted potatoes and a cup of tea. She saved the apples for Rudi. Hunger made her see him get up from his sickbed, harness the horses, and set out on his way.

Strange, she now remembered his gait even more than his face—not the gait of a Jew, but a broad, self-assured swagger.

After a few days of steady sleep he woke up and asked, "Where am I?"

"Here," said Arna, and she saw right away that the fog had lifted from his eyes, not entirely, but enough so that you could see the pupils. He was very thin, his brow was white, and on his right temple a yellow spot glowed.

"I've been asleep," he said.

"You slept well," she said.

"Where are the horses?" he remembered.

"Here," said Arna, pointing at them. "Aren't you cold?"

"No," he said and closed his eyes.

From time to time he would open them. Arna was sitting by his side, waiting for his eyes to open. The snowstorm died down, the sun broke in and flooded the ruin with light. It was a three-room house. A few shelves were still hanging in the kitchen.

How many days had passed since they'd gotten there? She had lost count. Now only two little apples were left. Not even a single potato. The hunger that had tormented her during the past few days stopped afflicting her. Her head was heavy. She sat without moving, drinking cold tea and hallucinating.

At some distance, on the main road, a sled would occasionally pass by, scattering the sound of its bells through the silent expanse. It was the ringing, more than any other contact, that brought images of her father and mother and her two little brothers before her eyes. It seemed to her they were still sitting on their bundles in that dark station.

Rudi woke up and said, "I'm hungry."

"I have nothing to give you. It's all gone." She knelt beside him.

The next day he tried to stand up. He leaned against the wall, and the white light outside whitened his face even more. His lips bit each other with the huge effort. At night a strong wind blew and broke up the snowdrifts. Occasionally a mass of snow would fall into the gutter and shake the walls.

They had no choice but to set out. The road was clear but twisting and encumbered with mud. The horses were weak and tried hard, but they could not advance. No houses were visible around them, only trees, patches of snow, and torrential rivers.

"Spring has come, unless I'm mistaken," Arna said to herself in surprise. Rudi was weak. The cold air weakened him even more. "I must get Rudi to shelter soon." Her hands hurried, but the horses were tired and did not draw the carriage.

The inn they reached at nightfall was completely full. Seeing the guests enter, a kind of neighing burst from the peasants' throats, the way they might greet a beast in its stable.

"Who are you?" asked the proprietor. Rudi showed him his papers, and he opened his eyes wide in surprise, as though he could not believe what he was seeing. The peasants reacted differently. The strange pair seemed suspicious to them, and they broke out in a mocking roar.

Rudi was furious, but he did not have the strength to raise his fists. He was fettered by his weakness and could only bite his tongue.

Arna was practical. She bought bread, cheese, smoked sausage. "My body, the devil take my body," Rudi thought, reviling his body, and they went out.

The snow melted and filled the air with pleasant humidity. A peephole opened in Rudi's memory. He saw his mother clearly, dressed in her winter coat, walking by his side. That bright image drew him out of his weakness for a moment. For

long hours they traveled without exchanging a word. Rudi's
visions overcame him, doing whatever they wished. Finally
hunger decided for them, and they stopped the wagon.

Arna was pleased that she could give him peasant bread
and white cheese. Immediately after the meal he fell asleep.
She wrapped him in two blankets, and he did not move until
morning.

Between one cold wave and the next the sun would descend and bathe the earth with its warmth. The earth was
peaceful and exhaled thick mist.

"Thank you, Arna," he said softly.

"Why are you thanking me?"

"For curing me."

"I didn't do anything special," she said without moving
her hands.

He sat and looked at her: small, thin, in a dress that had
fallen into tatters around her as if she were a servant, or rather
a servant's daughter: uprightness and submissiveness together.

He imagined that Arna's house was a poor one, clean, and
that faith permeated every corner of it. The truth, of course,
was quite different. Her father was not religious. He used to
make a fuss about anything that smacked of religion: it was
forbidden to say "Thank God" or "Praise the Lord." Her mother
secretly retained her faith, and in secret she had taught Arna
to recite "Hear, O Israel."

Meanwhile they ran out of food. They had no money, and
they sold clothes. His heart would cringe at the sight of one
of his mother's dresses, which were not merely objects for him,
but visions endowed with seasons, rooms, and balconies, his
mother in the brown wool dress, in the green silk dress, sitting
in the armchair or leaning against the wall. The peasant women,
of course, could not read the names of the famous wool mer-

chants. After bargaining briefly they would stuff the dresses into a sack like old sheets or tattered blankets.

Early that spring he thought a lot about his physical weakness, his mother, his Jewishness, and his fate in that green wilderness. But more than anything Arna amazed him. Every day he found a new virtue in her. One evening he revealed to her, "My father wasn't a Jew."

"But your mother was."

"Correct."

"Does it bother you?"

"Yes, to tell the truth."

"Don't worry," she spoke with assurance.

Now it was clear to him, her small body bore many secrets within it, hidden secrets. He would have to learn from her as long as he lived. At their stopovers he would sit across from her and ask her questions. Strangely she was not embarrassed. "Arna is not afraid of death," he said to himself.

The snow kept melting. Occasionally a stone or an iron bar would land on the carriage. He did not have the strength to run after them. He would bite his lips in anger. Arna's reaction was different: "Gentiles will always be gentiles."

"How is that?" he tried to understand.

"Uncircumcised heathen," she whispered. "Father would not use that word. He forbade us to use it. Once, I remember, he got very angry, and in his fury he cried out: 'Silence, woman!' "

"I only saw my father once."

"Was he hard?" she found no other words.

"I would say he was coarse."

Arna smiled as though hearing words not used in polite company.

They passed from hill to hill. Rudi's faculties returned to

him slightly, and he could stand up. He would sit and make
the fire and see to it that the flame was blue and effective. For
his mother's lovely dresses they received comestibles, not many,
and not particularly fresh. He knew there was no choice, and
did not grumble.

"What's my mother doing now?"

"She's certainly expecting you."

Arna only spoke about herself if asked. She was completely given over to his health. His recovery made her happy.
But the peasants looked unfavorably on their wandering existence. They assaulted them at every bend in the road and
beside every well like wild beasts smelling weakness. They would
take whatever they could grab, a blanket, a dress, or a utensil.
Rudi knew shouts would be of no help, and his body was too
weak to do battle.

"That's how the goyim are. We must seek Jews. It's better
to be with Jews."

Occasionally, as skittish as the breeze, the shadow of a
woman or child would flit past them. Arna knew they were
Jews, they were so thin, and they did not dare to stop. Rudi
too reached the conclusion that only Jews would protect Arna.
She was as slight as a baby chick and it would be best to seek
shelter with them soon. His own existence no longer concerned him. But where were the Jews? Where had they disappeared to? The little railway stations were now idle and
empty. From time to time an express train would pass by them,
emitting a frightful whistle.

Arna was firm in her resolve that he had to eat dairy prod-
ucts. She believed that cheese would cure him. She could not
be swayed. And he, like a boy who has been reprimanded, ate
everything she gave him.

"Do you believe in God?" she surprised him.

"I don't know."

"You should believe."

"You're right."

Every day she amazed him more. In her voice he imagined that he heard a message from the hidden worlds he used to envision during his childhood, when he heard music. In recent years he had not listened to music, and the colorful visions had disappeared as if of their own accord.

They wandered from place to place and sought Jews, they looked in every ruin and pit. At night Arna would press her ear to the ground, perhaps she would hear a familiar voice. The shadows that fluttered by them did not stop. The ones who did approach were the peasants. They would walk up to the trunk and snatch whatever came to hand, like hyenas.

They wandered northward. The horses weakened. Even a small burden was troublesome for them. How young and firm they had been when they were bought! They had aged during the past few months. A human sadness clung to their long faces. If it weren't for the peasants they would have nestled in one of the ravines and waited. Arna's heart told her that they would find Jews only at a railway station.

"How do you know?" he asked in surprise.

"I smell Jewish clothes there."

"And here there are none?"

"No. Only the smell of cows and horses."

He himself did not know how much he had changed. He was completely enthralled by Arna's charms. Every word and gesture moved him and made him marvel.

"And we'll find them all there?" he asked, testing her.

"Without doubt," Arna said with assurance.

Those days, the last in that landscape, brought him pleasures he had not known. The bread, the cheese, and the light, and a kind of excitement as though before a long voyage. He lost his former essence. Astonishment filled his soul.

Arna's spirit was calm. She did the many chores quietly, without extra motion. She even washed a shirt at night. The springtime shed its grace on them. Rudi gained strength.

"Soon we'll find them all."

"How do you know?"

"At night I saw my mother, and she was very pleased. Do you dream?"

"No."

"Too bad. So you have no contact with your mother."

"No. Since I lost her, I haven't seen her except in waking dreams."

"That's good. Hold onto that."

At one point Arna baked an apple cake. The cake was burned at the edges, but it was very tasty. Rudi did not stop praising her deeds.

The spring brought the peasants out of their huts and into the fields. They were tall peasants who threw stones and iron bars at them, shouting loudly: "Death to the Jews! Death to the merchants!" Only at night, only in the ravines, would Rudi halt the carriage to bind the horses' bleeding legs.

"That's how it is," Arna said, "Toward the end, the journey is always hard."

"Toward what end?" he tried to understand.

"Until you get there. We mustn't be discouraged. Mommy always said, you mustn't be discouraged. It's a sin to be discouraged."

"How's that?"

"God is very great."

He was surprised for a moment by the word *great* but he asked no more questions. As if he understood that one doesn't probe a secret. At dawn Rudi took a gold pendant out of the bag and presented it to Arna.

"What's this?" Arna asked, her hands shaking.

"It's my mother's pendant. Put it around your neck."

"I don't wear jewelry. My mother didn't wear jewelry."

"It will look good on you, you'll see."

Arna put it around her neck. She, of course, did not know its value, and Rudi didn't bother to tell her. In his heart he was pleased that one of his mother's things hung around her neck.

Before two days passed they reached a railroad station. It was a small, remote station, wrapped in heavy pines. There was no marker or sign indicating that it was a station, but Arna guessed it was, and she was drawn to the place.

"There they are!" she called out.

"You're right," Rudi agreed. "Why didn't I see them?"

Close by, an old policeman sat on a chair and smoked a pipe.

It was an old-fashioned rural railway station where lumber was loaded and unloaded, where the express would pass by without stopping. The local came but once a day, in the evening. Tears streamed from her eyes.

"What will we do with the horses?" Rudi asked for some reason.

"We'll leave them here. No one will take them."

"True," said Rudi, and immediately he was sorry to have raised such a trivial matter at an emotional moment.

No one rose to greet them. The people were sitting next to their bundles. A kind of gray chill left over from winter stood in the air. It turned out that two days before the police had tried to crowd them all into a railroad car, but the car was full, and they were ejected. Since then they had been here, separated from their loved ones, forgotten, waiting for a train to come and take them.

"And you?" one of the women asked Arna.

She wanted to say, "We were looking for you," but she said, "We didn't know what to do, so we came here."

"Sit down, children, sit down," said the woman in domestic tones. "Where are you from?"

"I'm from here," Arna said. "I lost my parents and my two little brothers. I'm looking for them."

"They're all on their way by now," said the woman. "Only we are here, forsaken." She was about thirty-five, and you could tell she had grayed during the past few days.

One of the women there spanked her little boy, hard. He wailed and brayed heavily.

"You're strangling him," said another woman, distractedly.

"He's driving me crazy."

"Explain it to him. He'll understand. He's a big boy."

"I explained. He's dumb."

The boy, about seven, stopped his wailing. His full, round face looked dull. His mother ignored him, and he sat on a package and nibbled a piece of bread.

"Where is the young man from?" the woman addressed Arna.

"From Austria. He lost his mother on the way. Now he's looking for her."

"We all speak German," the woman turned to Rudi. "This region used to belong to Austria." As she spoke it was as if her face was restored to her. She continued, "I myself studied German with a private tutor: grammar and literature. The locals don't speak German, only we. From Vienna, yes?"

"Not far."

"All my life I wanted to get to Vienna. I doubt that I'll make it. Children didn't grow up easily." Directly she regretted that confession and added, "Thou shalt eat bread by the sweat of thy brow." Like most of the girls, she had studied the Bible in German.

The woman took two sandwiches out of her handbag and offered one to Arna and one to Rudi. "Eat, children. You're probably hungry."

"Thank you," they said together.

"Who fed you?" the woman asked in an old, motherly tone.

"We ate whatever there was, we didn't go hungry, thank God," said Arna.

The people sat quietly on their bundles. If it hadn't been for the few children, not a sound would have been heard. The boy who had been spanked now sat forgotten beside his mother, gazing off at some distant point. With great effort his mother tied a cord around a heavy parcel.

"What do you think you'll do?" the woman asked them.

"We'll go with everyone else. What can we do?"

"They took my two daughters from me. I don't know when I'll see them again. They pushed everyone in, and I didn't manage to get pushed. I'm stupid. I'm completely stupid."

"In a little while you'll meet again, a little while," Arna whispered.

"But in the meantime, who will feed them? The big one is eight, and the little one is six."

"People will help them, just as you help," Arna said.

Strangely that sentence calmed the woman down for a moment. She shut her eyes, and a smile flitted across her tired face.

"Strange that they forgot us," the woman looked up.

"You saw for yourself, the trains are overloaded," the woman next to her spoke up with a dry and alarmingly matter-of-fact voice.

Later on two old peasant women came and spread out their wares on sacks. The people traded their clothes for bread, cheese, and apples. The scattered apples reminded him, as if by magic, of his native city, of the school and of his house. An old, repressed anger, which he had never before released, swelled and rose within him. Now he remembered that his mother, when he was only six, fooled him and went out by the back door. He had cried and plunged a fork into his hand.

His mother, when she had returned late that night, had been sure the nanny had not watched over him properly. Outraged she had fired her on the spot. He was sorry that just now the old story had arisen and clouded his spirits. "Always those grim memories," the words slipped out of his mouth.

"What did you say?" Arna asked.

"Pardon me. I didn't mean to."

People gave them whatever was in their packages: slices of bread spread with butter and prune jam. Hands vied with one another in the darkness: who would give more? Rudi was hungry. He found the homemade food tasty, and he ate for a long while. After the meal he leaned against the wall and dozed off. The evening fell, and he did not notice. Meanwhile Arna managed to water the horses and give them the last bits of oats remaining in the box.

When Rudi woke up, darkness had already spread to every corner. People sat and smoked cigarettes. The woman sitting near them said, "Allow me to introduce myself. My name is Rosa Krantz."

It seemed as if she were about to address them, saying, "Please have a seat, why don't you sit near the window?" as she was certainly used to saying. She did get to her feet with a somewhat theatrical movement, saying, "For years, since the death of my husband, I have wanted to leave this province and I never managed. Rather I never made an effort. After my husband died, I was depressed. The girls were little. Now I am paying the price.

"Where did you want to go?" asked Rudi.

"To Italy. In my youth I loved to paint. Some artists saw my work and foresaw a future for me, but marriage, making a living, and raising my daughters robbed me of my will. In fact, I didn't do enough. And you, what are you studying?"

"Me? I don't know yet."

"You must decide soon. Time does not stand still, to our regret. Suddenly you get up in the morning, and you're already thirty. All is lost."

"I'm seventeen," Rudi said.

"A fine age, unquestionably, but that age demands great decisions. I got married at that age, and thus my artistic career was doomed. One must not remain in the provinces. See what the provinces do, they devour their children."

"What's going to happen?" a tall man approached them. He seemed to be of noble lineage, a physician or professor, to judge by his hat.

"All will be well," said Rosa. "Why are you concerned, sir?"

"Where will that wellness come from?"

"From within us, from within us, of course."

The man was a bit taken aback by that and backed off, doffing his hat.

The night was clear, mild, and the people prepared coffee and ate sandwiches. There was plenty of tobacco, and they offered one another cigarettes, choice ones. In the corners voices reminisced about old times that, for some reason, found expression now.

Now, with a kind of swelling optimism, which reminded Rudi of his mother, Rosa spoke of Italy as if her failures and disappointments were forgotten. Rudi recognized those tones

from his childhood, and he was sad for a moment about that
handsome woman whose dreams had fallen by the wayside.
"All our precious things fall away from us," he murmured to
himself. As he said it he noticed that the pendant suited Arna's neck, and that sweetened his sadness slightly.

The night grew steadily clearer. The lights of the heavens
poured out, soft and comforting. Some people wore their heavy
coats though there was no need for them. The tall man of
noble lineage emitted a broken sigh. He did not mean to burden anyone with his sadness; it had burst out on its own.

"Who wants coffee?" a nearby voice was heard. It turned
out to belong to an old man of antiquated elegance who wished
to offer the people a hot drink in the middle of the night. He
did more than merely call out. He poured it into cups and
served it.

"Thank you very much," said Rosa, putting her hand out
to him.

"Think nothing of it," said the old man. "Coffee is good
at night."

The tall man bowed in the direction of the old one, took
the cup, and said, "I thank you with all my heart." The words
sounded like a benediction.

"Who else?" called the old man. He did not wait for an
answer. He took the empty cups to the pump and rinsed them.
The sight of the old man by the pump reminded Rudi of an
ancient monastery, with high walls and locked gates; at night
the monk would leave his cell and go to the pump in the
courtyard. The coffee revived Rosa. She spoke lofty words now
about great cities where culture resided in every corner. "One
walks in the street, and, with a swoop, it catches one up.
With a swoop," she repeated, as if she had finally found the
right word for an elusive concept.

After midnight the wind rose and bore the pungent odor

of damp wooden floors. It was utterly dark, and from the nearby village the sound of a horse's whinnying occasionally was heard. The old man's hands were full with his work. People sat on their bundles, drank coffee, and smoked cigarettes.

"I never tasted such good coffee in my life," said Rosa.

"Excellent," confirmed the tall man with a single word.

She had forgotten her daughters. She spoke now of her late husband, and in the gush of her words she said, "May he forgive me. I do not wish to grumble or speak ill of him. He was a good man. Everyone thought so. He wore himself out with hard labor. I don't understand to this day why he didn't let me study painting. If I had studied painting, I wouldn't be here. I would be living in Rome."

"Why Rome?" The tall man expressed his surprise in a restrained voice.

"There all of mankind's treasures are laid up, freedom, beauty, everything that is lacking here is found there."

"I understand," said the man and bent his head.

"You mean to say it isn't so?"

"I mean very little, Madam."

"Am I mistaken?" Rosa asked, abashed. "If I am mistaken, I take it back," she said, turning to those around her.

"You are right, Madam," said the tall man, trying to appease her. "I was talking to myself."

His voice did not appease her. A cloud descended on Rosa's face and darkened it. She sat on the bundle without saying another word. The tall man lit a cigarette and withdrew into the shadows. The lights in the sky grew steadily fainter, and heavy clumps of darkness fell beside the trees. The water pump was completely covered in darkness, as if by a heavy blanket. The horses standing near it dug and kneaded the earth with their forefeet, snorting with pleasure. "In a short time we'll free them," Rudi said to himself. "They'll head for open pastures." A kind of sadness, or rather self-pity, flooded his body.

"Did I say something foolish?" Rosa asked Arna.

"No. By no means."

"Then why is that man looking at me in contempt?"

"Everything was fine. You're mistaken."

"Nothing can be done. It's my fault. I'm stupid."

Rudi was quite familiar with that voice, the voice of melancholy. When her spirits fell, his mother used to deplore her own behavior, accuse herself, and bury her head in her pillow. Now he wanted to get up and stand at that woman's side, but his voice, as if he were in a deep sleep, was not with him.

For a moment it seemed as though the whole matter here, sitting and waiting, was nothing but an error. There were many pressing and practical issues that demanded attention. And here people were sitting idle and relaxing, eating without interruption and chattering. "It's a mistake, I tell you, a mistake," a short man with the look of a merchant got to his feet. "They'll send us back. What do they need us for? What good will we do them? Will we conquer Russia? Will we perform miracles? They'll send us back. Common sense dictates that they'll send us back." That voice had something simple and hardy about it.

Rudi looked at Arna's neck again. The pendant suited her. A few emotional words fluttered on his lips, but he did not say them. It was painfully clear that all those little lights, the shadows and the faces, would stay with him for many years, even when he was far away, on another continent. Without noticing what he was doing he took Arna's hand and pressed it to his lips.

The night flowed on, heads nodded with fatigue, words grew sparser, and Rosa burst into tears.

"Just three days ago I had two daughters and a home, now

I have nothing. That's all I had, and now I have nothing at all in this world."

"Why are you crying?" women said, hurrying over to her. "You aren't alone. It's nothing, only dreams. You shouldn't cry over nightmares."

"I'm afraid," Rosa clutched herself.

"There's nothing to be afraid of. You mustn't be afraid," the women scolded her.

Rosa buried her head in both hands and said, "Forgive me."

The darkness began to sink away. On the treetops a few weak scraps of light glowed, opening a peephole in the sky. "No one can take that beauty away from us," the thought occurred to Rudi's tired brain. The coffee had inspired optimism in him. Now he wanted to get up, to go over to the old man and express his thanks. His legs felt heavy, but he overcame it, rose, and went over. The old man was sitting in his place next to the hissing primus stove. "I wanted to thank you," Rudi said. "Your coffee brought us all back to life again."

"I am glad," said the old man. "Too bad I have no cakes. My wife bakes excellent cakes, dry cakes, but she was already sent off in the train."

"I thank you in everyone's name."

"I am happy to do it," said the old man, rousing. "I have plenty of coffee. Coffee is a superlative beverage, isn't it?"

That remark embarrassed Rudi. He was not used to speaking of coffee in such terms.

"A superlative beverage," the old man repeated, and it was evident that he had no better adjective to express all that was contained within the dusky liquid. "Where are you from?"

"Austria."

"We are Jews and will remain Jews," said the old man, raising the flame of the primus stove.

In the morning a quarrel over a seat broke out between two old women. The quarrel was short and sharp and lasted no more than a few minutes. The mother who had previously spanked her son sat and suddenly raised her long, hard hand against him again. The boy was astonished by the blow but did not utter a sound. "Now you understand?" she growled at him.

"Where will we be brought together?" a woman asked a man who was leaning against the wall.

"Not far," answered the man in complete distraction.

"If so, why aren't they coming to pick us up?"

"They'll come," said the man. "Don't worry."

"We haven't been forgotten? Are you sure?"

The man was about to answer when a long whistle was heard, a festive whistle, and they all stood up and shouted at once, "It came. At last it came!" The tall man with the noble lineage removed his hat like the Christians, placing it diagonally across his broad chest. The movement, which seemed habitual with him, suddenly inspired them all with a kind of gravity.

It was an old locomotive, drawing two old cars—the local, apparently. It went from station to station, scrupulously gathering up the remainder.

ABOUT THE AUTHOR

AHARON APPELFELD was born in 1932 in Czernovitz, Bukovina (now part of the USSR). His mother was killed by the Nazis, and he was deported at the age of eight to a concentration camp, from which he escaped. He spent the next three years in hiding in the Ukraine, and eventually joined the Russian army. After the war he made his way to Italy and, in 1946, to Palestine. He now lives in Jerusalem. Aharon Appelfeld's other works in English translation include *Badenheim 1939*, *The Age of Wonders*, *Tzili: The Story of a Life* and *The Retreat*. He is the recipient of the Israel Prize.